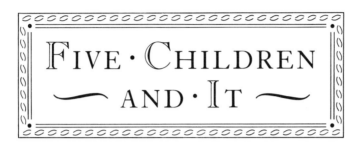

FIVE · CHILDREN — AND · IT —

FIVE · CHILDREN AND · IT

~ E . NESBIT ~

Illustrated by John Holder

BBC BOOKS

First published in hardback by BBC Books in 1990

This edition first published in paperback in 1992

BBC Books is a division of BBC Enterprises Limited,
Woodlands, 80 Wood Lane, London W12 0TT

Illustrations copyright © John Holder 1990

ISBN: 0 563 36398 3

Set by ACE Filmsetting Ltd, Frome
Printed and bound in Great Britain by Butler & Tanner Ltd, Frome
Colour separations by Technik Ltd, Berkhamsted
Cover printed by Clays Ltd, St Ives plc

TO JOHN BLAND

My Lamb, you are so very small,
You have not learned to read at all.
Yet never a printed book withstands
The urgence of your dimpled hands.
So, though this book is for yourself,
Let mother keep it on the shelf
Till you can read. O days that pass,
That day will come too soon, alas!

CONTENTS

LIST OF COLOUR ILLUSTRATIONS

Chapter I

BEAUTIFUL AS THE DAY

The house was three miles from the station, but before the dusty hired fly had rattled along for five minutes the children began to put their heads out of the carriage window to say, 'Aren't we nearly there?' And every time they passed a house, which was not very often, they all said, 'Oh, *is* this it?' But it never was, till they reached the very top of the hill, just past the chalk-quarry and before you come to the gravel-pit. And then there was a white house with a green garden and an orchard beyond, and Mother said, 'Here we are!'

'How white the house is,' said Robert.

'And look at the roses,' said Anthea.

'And the plums,' said Jane.

'It is rather decent,' Cyril admitted.

The Baby said, 'Wanty go walky'; and the fly stopped with a last rattle and a jolt.

Everyone got its legs kicked or its feet trodden on in the

scramble to get out of the carriage that very minute, but no one seemed to mind. Mother, curiously enough, was in no hurry to get out; and even when she had come down slowly and by the step, and with no jump at all, she seemed to wish to see the boxes carried in, and even to pay the driver, instead of joining in that first glorious rush round the garden and the orchard and the thorny, thistly, briery, brambly wilderness beyond the broken gate and the dry fountain at the side of the house. But the children were wiser, for once. It was not really a pretty house at all; it was quite ordinary, and Mother thought it was rather inconvenient, and was quite annoyed at there being no shelves, to speak of, and hardly a cupboard in the place. Father used to say that the ironwork on the roof and coping was like an architect's nightmare. But the house was deep in the country, with no other house in sight, and the children had been in London for two years, without so much as once going to the seaside even for a day by an excursion train, and so the White House seemed to them a sort of Fairy Palace set down in an Earthly Paradise. For London is like prison for children, especially if their relations are not rich.

Of course there are the shops and the theatres, and Maskelyne and Cook's, and things, but if your people are rather poor you don't get taken to the theatres, and you can't buy things out of the shops; and London has none of those nice things that children may play with without hurting the things or themselves – such as trees and sand and woods and waters. And nearly everything in London is the wrong sort of shape – all straight lines and flat streets, instead of being all sorts of odd shapes, like things are in the country. Trees are all different, as you know, and I am sure some tiresome person must have told you that there are no two blades of grass exactly alike. But in streets where the blades of grass don't grow, everything is like everything else. This is why so many children who live in towns are so extremely naughty. They do not know what is the matter with them, and no more do their fathers and mothers, aunts, uncles, cousins, tutors, governesses, and nurses; but I know. And so do you now. Children in the country are naughty sometimes, too, but that is for quite different reasons.

The children had explored the gardens and the outhouses thoroughly before they were caught and cleaned for tea, and they saw quite well that they were certain to be happy at the White House. They thought so from the first moment, but when they found the back of the house covered with jasmine, all in white flower, and smelling like a bottle of the most expensive scent that is ever given for a birthday present; and when they had seen the lawn, all green and smooth, and quite different from the brown grass in the gardens at Camden Town; and when they had found the stable with a loft over it and some old hay still left, they were almost certain; and when Robert had found the broken swing and tumbled out of it and got a lump on his head the size of an egg, and Cyril had nipped his finger in the door of a hutch that seemed made to keep rabbits in, if you ever had any, they had no longer any doubts whatever.

The best part of it all was that there were no rules about not going to places and not doing things. In London almost everything is labelled 'You mustn't touch', and though the label is invisible it's just as bad, because you know it's there, or if you don't you jolly soon get told.

The White House was on the edge of a hill, with a wood behind it – and the chalk-quarry on one side and the gravel-pit on the other. Down at the bottom of the hill was a level plain, with queer-shaped white buildings where people burnt lime, and a big red brewery and other houses; and when the big chimneys were smoking and the sun was setting, the valley looked as if it was filled with golden mist, and the limekilns and oast-houses glimmered and glittered till they were like an enchanted city out of the *Arabian Nights*.

Now that I have begun to tell you about the place, I feel that I could go on and make this into a most interesting story about all the ordinary things that the children did – just the kind of things you do yourself, you know – and you would believe every word of it; and when I told about the children's being tiresome, as you are sometimes, your aunts would perhaps write in the margin of the story with a pencil, 'How true!' or 'How like life!' and you would see it and very likely be annoyed. So I will only tell you the really astonishing things that happened, and you may leave the book about quite safely, for no aunts and uncles either are likely to write 'How true!' on the edge of the story. Grown-up people find it very difficult to believe really wonderful things, unless they have what they call proof. But children will believe almost anything, and grown-ups know this. That is why they tell you that the earth is round like an orange, when you can see perfectly well that it is flat and lumpy; and why they say that the earth goes round the sun, when you can see for yourself any day that the sun gets up in the morning and goes to bed at night like a good sun as it is, and the earth knows its place, and lies as still as a mouse. Yet I daresay you believe all that about the earth and the sun, and if so you will find it quite easy to believe that before Anthea and Cyril and the others had been a week in the country they had found a fairy. At least they called it that, because that was what it called itself; and of course it knew best, but it was not at all like any fairy you ever saw or heard of or read about.

It was at the gravel-pits. Father had to go away suddenly on business, and Mother had gone away to stay with Granny, who was not very well. They both went in a great hurry, and when they were gone the house seemed dreadfully quiet and empty, and the children wandered from one room to another and looked at the bits of paper and string on the floors left over from the packing, and not yet cleared up, and wished they had something to do. It was Cyril who said –

'I say, let's take our Margate spades and go and dig in the gravel-pits. We can pretend it's the seaside.'

'Father said it was once,' Anthea said; 'he says there are shells there thousands of years old.'

So they went. Of course they had been to the edge of the gravel-pit and looked over, but they had not gone down into it for fear Father should say they mustn't play there, and the same with the chalk-quarry. The gravel-pit is not really dangerous if you don't try to climb down the edges, but go the slow safe way round by the road, as if you were a cart.

Each of the children carried its own spade, and took it in turns to carry the Lamb. He was the baby, and they called him that because 'Baa' was the first thing he ever said. They called Anthea 'Panther', which seems silly when you read it, but when you say it it sounds a little like her name.

The gravel-pit is very large and wide, with grass growing round the edges at the top, and dry stringy wild flowers, purple and yellow. It is like a giant's wash-hand basin. And there are mounds of gravel, and holes in the sides of the basin where gravel has been taken out, and high up in the steep sides there are the little holes that are the little front doors of the little sand-martins' little houses.

The children built a castle, but castle-building is rather poor fun when you have no hope of the swishing tide ever coming in to fill up the moat and wash away the drawbridge, and, at the happy last, to wet everybody up to the waist at least.

Cyril wanted to dig out a cave to play smugglers in, but the others thought it might bury them alive, so it ended in all spades going to work to dig a hole through the castle to Australia. These children, you see, believed that the world was round, and that on the other side the little Australian boys and girls were really walking wrong way up, like flies on the ceiling, with their heads hanging down into the air.

The children dug and they dug and they dug, and their hands got sandy and hot and red, and their faces got damp and shiny. The Lamb had tried to eat the sand, and had cried so hard when he found out that it was not, as he had supposed, brown sugar, that he was now tired out, and was lying asleep in a warm fat bunch in the middle of the half-finished castle. This left his brothers and sisters free to work really hard, and the hole that was to come out in Australia soon grew so deep that Jane, who was called Pussy for short, begged the others to stop.

'Suppose the bottom of the hole gave way suddenly,' she said, 'and you tumbled out among the little Australians, all the sand would get in their eyes.'

'Yes,' said Robert; 'and they would hate us, and throw stones at us, and not let us see the kangaroos, or opossums, or blue-gums, or Emu Brand birds, or anything.'

Cyril and Anthea knew that Australia was not quite so near as all that, but they agreed to stop using their spades and go on with their hands. This was quite easy, because the sand at the bottom of the hole was very soft and fine and dry, like sea-sand. And there were little shells in it.

'Fancy it having been wet sea here once, all sloppy and shiny,' said Jane, 'with fishes and conger-eels and coral and mermaids.'

'And masts of ships and wrecked Spanish treasure. I wish we could find a gold doubloon, or something,' Cyril said.

'How did the sea get carried away?' Robert asked.

'Not in a pail, silly,' said his brother. 'Father says the earth got too hot underneath, like you do in bed sometimes, so it just hunched up its shoulders, and the sea had to slip off like the blankets do off us, and the shoulder was left sticking out, and turned into dry land. Let's go and look for shells; I think that little cave looks likely, and I see something sticking out there like a bit of wrecked ship's anchor, and it's beastly hot in the Australian hole.'

The others agreed, but Anthea went on digging. She always liked to finish a thing when she had once begun it. She felt it would be a disgrace to leave that hole without getting through to Australia.

The cave was disappointing, because there were no shells, and the wrecked ship's anchor turned out to be only the broken end of a pickaxe handle, and the cave party were just making up their minds that sand makes you thirstier when it is not by the seaside, and someone had suggested going home for lemonade, when Anthea suddenly screamed:

'Cyril! Come here! Oh, come quick! It's alive! It'll get away! Quick!'

They all hurried back.

'It's a rat, I shouldn't wonder,' said Robert. 'Father says they infest old places – and this must be pretty old if the sea was here thousands of years ago.'

'Perhaps it is a snake,' said Jane, shuddering.

'Let's look,' said Cyril, jumping into the hole. 'I'm not afraid of snakes. I like them. If it's a snake I'll tame it, and it will follow me everywhere, and I'll let it sleep round my neck at night.'

'No, you won't,' said Robert firmly. He shared Cyril's bed-room. 'But you may if it's a rat.'

'Oh, don't be silly!' said Anthea; 'it's not a rat, it's *much* bigger. And it's not a snake. It's got feet; I saw them; and fur! No – not the spade. You'll hurt it! Dig with your hands.'

'And let *it* hurt *me* instead! That's so likely, isn't it?' said Cyril, seizing a spade.

'Oh, don't!' said Anthea. 'Squirrel, *don't*. I – it sounds silly, but it said something. It really and truly did.'

'What?'

'It said, "You let me alone".'

But Cyril merely observed that his sister must have gone off her nut, and he and Robert dug with spades while Anthea sat on the edge of the hole, jumping up and down with hotness and anxiety. They dug carefully, and presently everyone could see that there really was something moving in the bottom of the Australian hole.

Then Anthea cried out. '*I'm* not afraid. Let me dig,' and fell on her knees and began to scratch like a dog does when he has suddenly remembered where it was that he buried his bone.

'Oh, I felt fur,' she cried, half laughing and half crying. 'I did indeed! I did!' when suddenly a dry husky voice in the sand made them all jump back, and their hearts jumped nearly as fast as they did.

'Let me alone,' it said. And now everyone heard the voice and looked at the others to see if they had too.

'But we want to see you,' said Robert bravely.

'I wish you'd come out,' said Anthea, also taking courage.

'Oh, well – if that's your wish,' the voice said, and the sand stirred and spun and scattered, and something brown and furry and fat came rolling out into the hole, and the sand fell off it, and it sat there yawning and rubbing the ends of its eyes with its hands.

'I believe I must have dropped asleep,' it said, stretching itself.

The children stood round the hole in a ring, looking at the creature they had found. It was worth looking at. Its eyes were on long horns like a snail's eyes, and it could move them in and out like telescopes; it had ears like a bat's ears, and its tubby body was shaped like a spider's and covered with thick soft fur; its legs and arms were furry too, and it had hands and feet like a monkey's.

'What on earth is it?' Jane said. 'Shall we take it home?'

The thing turned its long eyes to look at her, and said: 'Does she always talk nonsense, or is it only the rubbish on her head that makes her silly?'

It looked scornfully at Jane's hat as it spoke.

'She doesn't mean to be silly,' Anthea said gently; 'we none of us do, whatever you may think! Don't be frightened; we don't want to hurt you, you know.'

'Hurt *me*!' it said. '*Me* frightened! Upon my word! Why, you talk as if I were nobody in particular.' All its fur stood out like a cat's when it is going to fight.

'Well,' said Anthea, still kindly, 'perhaps if we knew who you are in particular we could think of something to say that wouldn't make you cross. Everything we've said so far seems to have. Who are you? And don't get angry! Because really we don't know.'

'You don't know?' it said. 'Well, I knew the world had changed – but – well, really – do you mean to tell me seriously you don't know a Psammead when you see one?'

'A Sammyadd? That's Greek to me.'

'So it is to everyone,' said the creature sharply. 'Well, in plain

English, then, a *Sand-fairy*. Don't you know a Sand-fairy when you see one?'

It looked so grieved and hurt that Jane hastened to say, 'Of course I see you are, *now*. It's quite plain now one comes to look at you.'

'You came to look at me several sentences ago,' it said crossly, beginning to curl up again in the sand.

'Oh – don't go away again! Do talk some more,' Robert cried. 'I didn't know you were a Sand-fairy, but I knew directly I saw you that you were much the wonderfullest thing I'd ever seen.'

The Sand-fairy seemed a shade less disagreeable after this.

'It isn't talking I mind,' it said, 'as long as you're reasonably civil. But I'm not going to make polite conversation for you. If you talk nicely to me, perhaps I'll answer you, and perhaps I won't. Now say something.'

Of course no one could think of anything to say, but at last Robert thought of 'How long have you lived here?' and he said it at once.

'Oh, ages – several thousand years,' replied the Psammead.

'Tell us about it. Do.'

'It's all in books.'

'*You* aren't!' Jane said. 'Oh, tell us everything you can about yourself! We don't know anything about you, and you *are* so nice.'

The Sand-fairy smoothed his long rat-like whiskers and smiled between them.

'Do please tell!' said all the children together.

It is wonderful how quickly you get used to things, even the most astonishing. Five minutes before, the children had had no more idea than you that there was such a thing as a sand-fairy in the world, and now they were talking to it as though they had known it all their lives.

It drew its eyes in and said:

'How very sunny it is – quite like old times. Where do you get your Megatheriums from now?'

'What?' said the children all at once. It is very difficult always to remember that 'what' is not polite, especially in moments of surprise or agitation.

'Are Pterodactyls plentiful now?' the Sand-fairy went on.

The children were unable to reply.

'What do you have for breakfast?' the Fairy said impatiently, 'and who gives it you?'

'Eggs and bacon, and bread-and-milk, and porridge and things. Mother gives it us. What are Mega-what's-it's-names and Ptero-what-do-you-call-thems? And does anyone have them for breakfast?'

'Why, almost everyone had Pterodactyl for breakfast in my time! Pterodactyls were something like crocodiles and something like birds – I believe they were very good grilled. You see, it was like this: of course there were heaps of sand-fairies then, and in the morning early you went out and hunted for them, and when you'd found one it gave you your wish. People used to send their little boys down to the seashore early in the morning before breakfast to get the day's wishes, and very often the eldest boy in the family would be told to wish for a Megatherium, ready jointed for cooking. It was as big as an elephant, you see, so there was a good deal of meat on it. And if they wanted fish, the Ichthyosaurus was asked for – he was twenty to forty feet long, so there was plenty of him. And for poultry there was the Plesiosaurus; there were nice pickings on that too. Then the other children could wish for other things. But when people had dinner-parties it was nearly always Megatheriums; and Ichthyosaurus, because his fins were a great delicacy and his tail made soup.'

'There must have been heaps and heaps of cold meat left over,' said Anthea, who meant to be a good housekeeper some day.

'Oh no,' said the Psammead, 'that would never have done. Why, of course at sunset what was left over turned into stone. You find the stone bones of the Megatherium and things all over the place even now, they tell me.'

'Who tell you?' asked Cyril; but the Sand-fairy frowned and began to dig very fast with its furry hands.

'Oh, don't go!' they all cried; 'tell us more about when it was Megatheriums for breakfast! Was the world like this then?'

It stopped digging.

'Not a bit,' it said; 'it was nearly all sand where I lived, and coal grew on trees, and the periwinkles were as big as tea-trays – you find them now; they're turned into stone. We sand-fairies used to live on the seashore, and the children used to come with their little flint-spades and flint-pails and make castles for us to live in. That's thousands of years ago, but I hear that children still build castles on the sand. It's difficult to break yourself of a habit.'

'But why did you stop living in the castles?' asked Robert.

'It's a sad story,' said the Psammead gloomily. 'It was because they *would* build moats to the castles, and the nasty wet bubbling sea used to come in, and of course as soon as a sand-fairy got wet it caught cold, and generally died. And so there got to be fewer and fewer, and, whenever you found a fairy and had a wish, you used to wish for a Megatherium, and eat twice as much as you wanted, because it might be weeks before you got another wish.'

'And did *you* get wet?' Robert inquired.

The Sand-fairy shuddered. 'Only once,' it said; 'the end of the twelfth hair of my top left whisker – I feel the place still in damp weather. It was only once, but it was quite enough for me. I went away as soon as the sun had dried my poor dear whisker. I scurried away to the back of the beach, and dug myself a house deep in warm dry sand, and there I've been ever since. And the sea changed its lodgings afterwards. And now I'm not going to tell you another thing.'

'Just one more, please,' said the children. 'Can you give wishes now?'

'Of course,' said it, 'didn't I give you yours a few minutes ago? You said, "I wish you'd come out," and I did.'

'Oh, please, mayn't we have another?'

'Yes, but be quick about it. I'm tired of you.'

I daresay you have often thought what you would do if you had three wishes given you, and have despised the old man and his wife in the black-pudding story, and felt certain that if you had the chance you could think of three really useful wishes without a moment's hesitation. These children had often talked this matter over, but, now the chance had suddenly come to them, they could not make up their minds.

'Quick,' said the Sand-fairy crossly. No one could think of anything, only Anthea did manage to remember a private wish of her own and Jane's which they had never told the boys. She knew the boys would not care about it – but still it was better than nothing.

'I wish we were all as beautiful as the day,' she said in a great hurry.

The children looked at each other, but each could see that the others were not any better-looking than usual. The Psammead pushed out its long eyes, and seemed to be holding its breath and swelling itself out till it was twice as fat and furry as before. Suddenly it let its breath go in a long sigh.

'I'm really afraid I can't manage it,' it said apologetically, 'I must be out of practice.'

The children were horribly disappointed.

'Oh, *do* try again!' they said.

'Well,' said the Sand-fairy, 'the fact is, I was keeping back a little strength to give the rest of you your wishes with. If you'll be contented with one wish a day amongst the lot of you I daresay I can screw myself up to do it. Do you agree to that?'

'Yes, oh yes!' said Jane and Anthea. The boys nodded. They did not believe the Sand-fairy could do it. You can always make girls believe things much easier than you can boys.

It stretched out its eyes farther than ever, and swelled and swelled and swelled.

'I do hope it won't hurt itself,' said Anthea.

'Or crack its skin,' said Robert anxiously.

Everyone was very much relieved when the Sand-fairy, after getting so big that it almost filled up the hole in the sand, suddenly let out its breath and went back to its proper size.

'That's all right,' it said, panting heavily. 'It'll come easier tomorrow.'

'Did it hurt much?' asked Anthea.

'Only my poor whisker, thank you,' said he, 'but you're a kind and thoughtful child. Good day.'

It scratched suddenly and fiercely with its hands and feet, and disappeared in the sand. Then the children looked at each other, and each child suddenly found itself alone with three perfect strangers, all radiantly beautiful.

They stood for some moments in perfect silence. Each thought that its brothers and sisters had wandered off, and that these strange children had stolen up unnoticed while it was watching the swelling form of the Sand-fairy. Anthea spoke first –

'Excuse me,' she said very politely to Jane, who now had enormous blue eyes and a cloud of russet hair, 'but have you seen two little boys and a little girl anywhere about?'

'I was just going to ask you that,' said Jane. And then Cyril cried:

'Why, it's *you*! I know the hole in your pinafore! You *are* Jane, aren't you? And you're the Panther; I can see your dirty handkerchief that you forgot to change after you'd cut your thumb! Crikey! The wish has come off, after all. I say, am I as handsome as you are?'

'If you're Cyril, I liked you better as you were before,' said Anthea decidedly. 'You look like the picture of the young chorister, with your golden hair; you'll die young, I shouldn't wonder. And if that's Robert, he's like an Italian organ-grinder. His hair's all black.'

'You two girls are like Christmas cards, then – that's all – silly Christmas cards,' said Robert angrily. 'And Jane's hair is simply carrots.'

It was indeed of that Venetian tint so much admired by artists.

'Well, it's no use finding fault with each other,' said Anthea; 'let's get the Lamb and lug it home to dinner. The servants will admire us most awfully, you'll see.'

Baby was just waking when they got to him, and not one of the children but was relieved to find that he at least was not as beautiful as the day, but just the same as usual.

'I suppose he's too young to have wishes naturally,' said Jane. 'We shall have to mention him specially next time.'

Anthea ran forward and held out her arms.

'Come to own Panther, ducky,' she said.

The Baby looked at her disapprovingly, and put a sandy pink thumb in his mouth. Anthea was his favourite sister.

'Come then,' she said.

'G'way long!' said the Baby.

'Come to own Pussy,' said Jane.

'Wants my Panty,' said the Lamb dismally, and his lip trembled.

'Here, come on, Veteran,' said Robert, 'come and have a yidey on Yobby's back.'

'Yah, narky narky boy,' howled the Baby, giving way altogether. Then the children knew the worst. *The Baby did not know them!*

They looked at each other in despair, and it was terrible to each, in this dire emergency, to meet only the beautiful eyes of perfect strangers, instead of the merry, friendly, commonplace, twinkling, jolly eyes of its own brothers and sisters.

'This is most truly awful,' said Cyril when he had tried to lift up the Lamb, and the Lamb had scratched like a cat and bellowed like a bull. 'We've got to *make friends* with him! I can't carry him home screaming like that. Fancy having to make friends with our own baby! – it's too silly.'

That, however, was exactly what they had to do. It took over an hour, and the task was not rendered any easier by the fact that the Lamb was by this time as hungry as a lion and as thirsty as a desert.

At last he consented to allow these strangers to carry him home by turns, but as he refused to hold on to such new aquaintances he was a dead weight, and most exhausting.

'Thank goodness, we're home!' said Jane, staggering through the iron gates to where Martha, the nursemaid, stood at the front door shading her eyes with her hand and looking out anxiously. 'Here! Do take Baby!'

Martha snatched the Baby from her arms.

'Thanks be, *he's* safe back,' she said. 'Where are the others, and whoever to goodness gracious are all of you?'

'We're *us*, of course,' said Robert.

'And who's *us*, when you're at home?' asked Martha scornfully.

'I tell you it's *us*, only we're beautiful as the day,' said Cyril. 'I'm Cyril, and these are the others, and we're jolly hungry. Let us in, and don't be a silly idiot.'

Martha merely dratted Cyril's impudence and tried to shut the door in his face.

'I know we *look* different, but I'm Anthea, and we're so tired, and it's long past dinner-time.'

'Then go home to your dinners, whoever you are; and if our children put you up to this play-acting you can tell them from me they'll catch it, so they know what to expect!' With that she did bang the door. Cyril rang the bell violently. No answer. Presently cook put her head out of a bedroom window and said:

'If you don't take yourself off, and that precious sharp, I'll go and fetch the police.' And she slammed down the window.

'It's no good,' said Anthea. 'Oh, do, do come away before we get sent to prison!'

The boys said it was nonsense, and the law of England couldn't put you in prison for just being as beautiful as the day, but all the same they followed the others out into the lane.

'We shall be our proper selves after sunset, I suppose,' said Jane.

'I don't know,' Cyril said sadly; 'it mayn't be like that now – things have changed a good deal since Megatherium times.'

'Oh,' cried Anthea suddenly, 'perhaps we shall turn into stone at sunset, like the Megatheriums did, so that there mayn't be any of us left over for the next day.'

She began to cry, so did Jane. Even the boys turned pale. No one had the heart to say anything.

It was a horrible afternoon. There was no house near where the children could beg a crust of bread or even a glass of water. They were afraid to go to the village, because they had seen Martha go down there with a basket, and there was a local constable. True, they were all as beautiful as the day, but that is a poor comfort when you are as hungry as a hunter and as thirsty as a sponge.

Three times they tried in vain to get the servants in the White House to let them in and listen to their tale. And then Robert went alone, hoping to be able to climb in at one of the back windows and so open the door to the others. But all the windows were out of reach, and Martha emptied a toilet-jug of cold water over him from a top window, and said:

'Go along with you, you nasty little Eyetalian monkey.'

It came at last to their sitting down in a row under the hedge, with their feet in a dry ditch, waiting for sunset, and wondering whether, when the sun *did* set, they would turn to stone, or only into their own natural selves; and each of them still felt lonely and among strangers and tried not to look at the others, for, though their voices were their own, their faces were so radiantly beautiful as to be quite irritating to look at.

'I don't believe we *shall* turn to stone,' said Robert, breaking a long miserable silence, 'because the Sand-fairy said he'd give us another wish tomorrow, and he couldn't if we were stone, could he?'

The others said 'No,' but they weren't at all comforted.

Another silence, longer and more miserable, was broken by

Cyril's suddenly saying, 'I don't want to frighten you girls, but I believe it's beginning with me already. My foot's quite dead. I'm turning to stone, I know I am, and so will you in a minute.'

'Never mind,' said Robert kindly, 'perhaps you'll be the only stone one, and the rest of us will be all right, and we'll cherish your statue and hang garlands on it.'

But when it turned out that Cyril's foot had only gone to sleep through his sitting too long with it under him, and when it came to life in an agony of pins and needles, the others were quite cross.

'Giving us such a fright for nothing!' said Anthea.

The third and miserablest silence of all was broken by Jane. She said: 'If we *do* come out of this all right we'll ask the Sammyadd to make it so that the servants don't notice anything different, no matter what wishes we have.'

The others only grunted. They were too wretched even to make good resolutions.

At last hunger and fright and crossness and tiredness – four very nasty things – all joined together to bring one nice thing, and that was sleep. The children lay asleep in a row, with their beautiful eyes shut and their beautiful mouths open. Anthea woke first. The sun had set, and the twilight was coming on.

Anthea pinched herself very hard, to make sure, and when she found she could still feel pinching she decided that she was not stone, and then she pinched the others. They, also, were soft.

'Wake up,' she said, almost in tears for joy; 'it's all right, we're not stone. And oh, Cyril, how nice and ugly you do look, with your old freckles and your brown hair and your little eyes. And so do you all!' she added, so that they might not feel jealous.

When they got home they were very much scolded by Martha, who told them about the strange children.

'A good-looking lot, I must say, but that impudent.'

'I know,' said Robert, who knew by experience how hopeless it would be to try to explain things to Martha.

'And where on earth have you been all this time, you naughty little things, you?'

'In the lane.'

'Why didn't you come home hours ago?'

'We couldn't because of *them*,' said Anthea.

'Who?'

'The children who were as beautiful as the day. They kept us there till after sunset. We couldn't come back till they'd gone. You don't know how we hated them! Oh, do, do give us some supper – we are so hungry.'

'Hungry! I should think so,' said Martha angrily; 'out all day like this. Well, I hope it'll be a lesson to you not to go picking up with strange children – down here after measles, as likely as not. Now mind, if you see them again, don't speak to them – not one word nor so much as a look – but come straight away and tell me. I'll spoil their beauty for them!'

'If ever we *do* see them again we'll tell you,' Anthea said; and Robert, fixing his eyes fondly on the cold beef that was being brought in on a tray by the cook, added in heartfelt undertones –

'And we'll take jolly good care we never *do* see them again.'

And they never have.

It stretched out its eyes farther than ever, and swelled and swelled and swelled

And all the gleaming heap was minted gold

GOLDEN GUINEAS

Anthea woke in the morning from a very real sort of dream, in which she was walking in the Zoological Gardens on a pouring wet day without any umbrella. The animals seemed desperately unhappy because of the rain, and were all growling gloomily. When she awoke, both the growling and the rain went on just the same. The growling was the heavy regular breathing of her sister Jane, who had a slight cold and was still asleep. The rain fell in slow drops on to Anthea's face from the wet corner of a bath-towel which her brother Robert was gently squeezing the water out of, to wake her up, as he now explained.

'Oh, drop it!' she said rather crossly; so he did, for he was not a brutal brother, though very ingenious in apple-pie beds, booby-traps, original methods of awakening sleeping relatives, and the other little accomplishments which made home happy.

'I had such a funny dream,' Anthea began.

'So did I,' said Jane, wakening suddenly and without warning.

'I dreamed we found a Sand-fairy in the gravel-pits, and it said it was a Sammyadd, and we might have a new wish every day, and –'

'But that's what *I* dreamed,' said Robert; 'I was just going to tell you – and we had the first wish directly it said so. And I dreamed you girls were donkeys enough to ask for us all to be beautiful as the day, and we jolly well were, and it was perfectly beastly.'

'But *can* different people all dream the same thing?' said Anthea, sitting up in bed, 'because I dreamed all that as well as about the Zoo and the rain; and Baby didn't know us in my dream, and the servants shut us out of the house because the radiantness of our beauty was such a complete disguise, and –'

The voice of the eldest brother sounded from across the landing.

'Come on, Robert,' it said, 'you'll be late for breakfast again – unless you mean to shirk your bath like you did on Tuesday.'

'I say, come here a sec,' Robert replied. 'I didn't shirk it; I had it after brekker in father's dressing-room, because ours was emptied away.'

Cyril appeared in the doorway, partially clothed.

'Look here,' said Anthea, 'we've all had such an odd dream. We've all dreamed we found a Sand-fairy.'

Her voice died away before Cyril's contemptuous glance. 'Dream?' he said; 'you little sillies, it's *true*. I tell you it all happened. That's why I'm so keen on being down early. We'll go there directly after brekker, and have another wish. Only we'll make up our minds, solid, before we go, what it is we do want, and no one must ask for anything unless the others agree first. No more peerless beauties for this child, thank you. Not if I know it!'

The other three dressed, with their mouths open. If all that dream about the Sand-fairy was real, this real dressing seemed very like a dream, the girls thought. Jane felt that Cyril was right, but Anthea was not sure, till after they had seen Martha and heard her full and plain reminders about their naughty conduct the day before. Then Anthea was sure. 'Because,' said she, 'servants never dream anything but the things in the *Dream-book*, like snakes and oysters and going to a wedding – that means a funeral, and snakes are a false female friend, and oysters are babies.'

'Talking of babies,' said Cyril, 'where's the Lamb?'

'Martha's going to take him to Rochester to see her cousins. Mother said she might. She's dressing him now,' said Jane, 'in his very best coat and hat. Bread-and-butter, please.'

'She seems to like taking him too,' said Robert in a tone of wonder.

'Servants do like taking babies to see their relations,' Cyril said; 'I've noticed it before – especially in their best things.'

'I expect they pretend they're their own babies, and that they're not servants at all, but married to noble dukes of high degree, and they say the babies are the little dukes and duchesses,' Jane suggested dreamily, taking more marmalade. 'I expect that's what Martha'll say to her cousin. She'll enjoy herself most frightfully.'

'She won't enjoy herself most frightfully carrying our infant duke to Rochester,' said Robert; 'not if she's anything like me – she won't.'

'Fancy walking to Rochester with the Lamb on your back! Oh, crikey!' said Cyril in full agreement.

'She's going by carrier,' said Jane. 'Let's see them off, then we shall have done a polite and kindly act, and we shall be quite sure we've got rid of them for the day.'

So they did.

Martha wore her Sunday dress of two shades of purple, so tight in the chest that it made her stoop, and her blue hat with the pink cornflowers and white ribbon. She had a yellow-lace collar with a green bow. And the Lamb had indeed his very best cream-coloured silk coat and hat. It was a smart party that the carrier's cart picked up at the Cross Roads. When its white tilt and red wheels had slowly vanished in a swirl of chalk-dust –

'And now for the Sammyadd!' said Cyril, and off they went.

As they went they decided on the wish they would ask for. Although they were in a great hurry they did not try to climb down the sides of the gravel-pit, but went round by the safe lower road, as if they had been carts. They had made a ring of stones round the place where the Sand-fairy had disappeared, so they easily found the spot. The sun was burning and bright, and the sky was deep blue – without a cloud. The sand was very hot to touch.

'Oh – suppose it was only a dream, after all,' Robert said as the boys uncovered their spades from the sand-heap where they had buried them and began to dig.

'Suppose you were a sensible chap,' said Cyril; 'one's quite as likely as the other!'

'Suppose you kept a civil tongue in your head,' Robert snapped.

'Suppose we girls take a turn,' said Jane, laughing. 'You boys seem to be getting very warm.'

'Suppose you don't come shoving your silly oar in,' said Robert, who was now warm indeed.

'We won't,' said Anthea quickly. 'Robert dear, don't be so grumpy – we won't say a word, you shall be the one to speak to the Fairy and tell him what we've decided to wish for. You'll say it much better than we shall.'

'Suppose you drop being a little humbug,' said Robert, but not crossly. 'Look out – dig with your hands, now!'

So they did, and presently uncovered the spider-shaped brown hairy body, long arms and legs, bat's ears and snail's eyes of the Sand-fairy himself. Everyone drew a deep breath of satisfaction, for now of course it couldn't have been a dream.

The Psammead sat up and shook the sand out of its fur.

'How's your left whisker this morning?' said Anthea politely.

'Nothing to boast of,' said it; 'it had rather a restless night. But thank you for asking.'

'I say,' said Robert, 'do you feel up to giving wishes today, because we very much want an extra besides the regular one? The extra's a very little one,' he added reassuringly.

'Humph!' said the Sand-fairy. (If you read this story aloud, please pronounce 'humph' exactly as it is spelt, for that is how he said it.) 'Humph! Do you know, until I heard you being disagreeable to each other just over my head, and so loud too, I really quite thought I had dreamed you all. I do have very odd dreams sometimes.'

'Do you?' Jane hurried to say, so as to get away from the subject of disagreeableness. 'I wish,' she added politely, 'you'd tell us about your dreams – they must be awfully interesting.'

'Is that the day's wish?' said the Sand-fairy, yawning.

Cyril muttered something about 'just like a girl', and the rest stood silent. If they said 'Yes,' then good-bye to the other wishes they had decided to ask for. If they said 'No,' it would be very rude, and they had all been taught manners, and had learned a little too, which is not at all the same thing. A sigh of relief broke from all lips when the Sand-fairy said:

'If I do I shan't have strength to give you a second wish; not even good tempers, or common sense, or manners, or little things like that.'

'We don't want you to put yourself out at all about *these* things, we can manage them quite well ourselves,' said Cyril eagerly; while the others looked guiltily at each other, and wished the Fairy would not keep all on about good tempers, but give them one good rowing if it wanted to, and then have done with it.

'Well,' said the Psammead, putting out his long snail's eyes so suddenly that one of them nearly went into the round boy's eye of Robert, 'let's have the little wish first.'

'We don't want the servants to notice the gifts you give us.'

'Are kind enough to give us,' said Anthea in a whisper.

'Are kind enough to give us, I mean,' said Robert.

The Fairy swelled himself out a bit, let his breath go, and said –

'I've done *that* for you – it was quite easy. People don't notice things much, anyway. What's the next wish?'

'We want,' said Robert slowly, 'to be rich beyond the dreams of something or other.'

'Avarice,' said Jane.

'So it is,' said the Fairy unexpectedly. 'But it won't do you much good, that's one comfort,' it muttered to itself. 'Come – I can't go beyond dreams, you know! How much do you want, and will you have it in gold or notes?'

'Gold, please – and millions of it.'

'This gravel-pit full be enough?' said the Fairy in an offhand manner.

'Oh *yes*!'

'Then get out before I begin, or you'll be buried alive in it.'

It made its skinny arms so long, and waved them so frighteningly, that the children ran as hard as they could towards the road by which carts used to come to the gravel-pits. Only Anthea had the presence of mind to shout a timid 'Good-morning, I hope your whisker will be better tomorrow,' as she ran.

On the road they turned and looked back, and they had to shut their eyes, and open them very slowly, a little bit at a time, because the sight was too dazzling for their eyes to be able to bear it. It was something like trying to look at the sun at high noon on Midsummer Day. For the whole of the sand-pit was full, right up to the very top, with new shining gold pieces, and all the little sand-martins' little front doors were covered out of sight. Where the road for the carts wound into the gravel-pit the gold lay in heaps like stones lie by the roadside, and a great bank of shining gold shelved down from where it lay flat and smooth between the tall sides of the gravel-pit. And all the gleaming heap was minted gold. And on the sides and edges of these countless coins the midday sun shone and sparkled, and glowed and gleamed till the quarry looked like the mouth of a smelting furnace, or one of the fairy halls that you see sometimes in the sky at sunset.

The children stood with their mouths open, and no one said a word.

At last Robert stooped and picked up one of the loose coins from the edge of the heap by the cart-road, and looked at it. He looked on both sides. Then he said in a low voice, quite different to his own, 'It's not sovereigns.'

'It's gold, anyway,' said Cyril. And now they all began to talk at once. They all picked up the golden treasure by handfuls and let it run through their fingers like water, and the chink it made as it fell was wonderful music. At first they quite forgot to think of spending the money, it was so nice to play with. Jane sat down between two heaps of gold, and Robert began to bury her, as you bury your father in sand when you are at the seaside and he has gone to sleep on the beach with his newspaper over his face. But Jane was not half buried before she cried out, 'Oh, stop, it's too heavy! It hurts!'

Robert said 'Bosh!' and went on.

'Let me out, I tell you,' cried Jane, and was taken out, very white, and trembling a little.

'You've no idea what it's like,' she said; 'it's like stones on you – or like chains.'

'Look here,' Cyril said, 'if this is to do us any good, it's no good our staying gasping at it like this. Let's fill our pockets and go and buy things. Don't you forget, it won't last after sunset. I wish we'd asked the Sammyadd why things don't turn to stone. Perhaps this will. I'll tell you what, there's a pony and cart in the village.'

'Do you want to buy that?' asked Jane.

'No, silly – we'll *hire* it. And then we'll go to Rochester and buy heaps and heaps of things. Look here, let's each take as much as we can carry. But it's not sovereigns. They've got a man's head on one side and a thing like the ace of spades on the other. Fill your pockets with it, I tell you, and come along. You can jaw as we go – if you *must* jaw!'

Cyril sat down and began to fill his pockets.

'You made fun of me for getting Father to have nine pockets in my Norfolks,' said he, 'but now you see!'

They did. For when Cyril had filled his nine pockets and his handkerchief and the space between himself and his shirt front with the gold coins, he had to stand up. But he staggered, and had to sit down again in a hurry.

'Throw out some of the cargo,' said Robert. 'You'll sink the ship, old chap. That comes of nine pockets.'

And Cyril had to.

Then they set off to walk to the village. It was more than a mile, and the road was very dusty indeed, and the sun seemed to get hotter and hotter, and the gold in their pockets got heavier and heavier.

It was Jane who said, 'I don't see how we're going to spend it all. There must be thousands of pounds among the lot of us. I'm going to leave some of mine behind this stump in the hedge. And directly we get to the village we'll buy some biscuits; I know it's long past dinner-time.' She took out a handful or two of gold and hid it in the hollows of an old hornbeam. 'How round and yellow they are,' she said. 'Don't you wish they were gingerbread nuts and we were going to eat them?'

'Well, they're not, and we're not,' said Cyril. 'Come on!'

But they came on heavily and wearily. Before they reached the village, more than one stump in the hedge concealed its little hoard of hidden treasure. Yet they reached the village with about twelve hundred guineas in their pockets. But in spite of this inside wealth they looked quite ordinary outside, and no one would have thought they could have more than a half-crown each at the outside. The haze of heat, the blue of the wood smoke, made a sort of dim misty cloud over the red roofs of the village. The four sat down heavily on the first bench they came to. It happened to be outside the Blue Boar Inn.

It was decided that Cyril should go into the Blue Boar and ask for ginger-beer, because, as Anthea said, 'It is not wrong for men to go into public houses, only for children. And Cyril is nearer to being a man than us, because he is the eldest.' So he went. The others sat in the sun and waited.

'Oh, hats, how hot it is!' said Robert. 'Dogs put their tongues out when they're hot; I wonder if it would cool us at all to put out ours?'

'We might try,' Jane said; and they all put their tongues out as far as ever they could go, so that it quite stretched their throats, but it only seemed to make them thirstier than ever, besides annoying everyone who went by. So they took their tongues in again, just as Cyril came back with the ginger-beer.

'I had to pay for it out of my own two-and-sevenpence, though, that I was going to buy rabbits with,' he said. 'They wouldn't change the gold. And when I pulled out a handful the man just laughed and said it was card-counters. And I got some sponge-cakes too, out of a glass jar on the bar-counter. And some biscuits with caraways in.'

The sponge-cakes were both soft and dry and the biscuits were dry too, and yet soft, which biscuits ought not to be. But the ginger-beer made up for everything.

'It's my turn now to try to buy something with the money,' Anthea said; 'I'm next eldest. Where is the pony-cart kept?'

It was at The Chequers, and Anthea went in the back way to the yard, because they all knew that little girls ought not to go into the bars of public-houses. She came out, as she herself said, 'pleased but not proud'.

'He'll be ready in a brace of shakes, he says,' she remarked, and he's to have one sovereign – or whatever it is – to drive us in to Rochester and back, besides waiting there till we've got everything we want. I think I managed very well.'

'You think yourself jolly clever, I daresay,' said Cyril moodily. 'How did you do it?'

'I wasn't jolly clever enough to go taking handfuls of money out of my pocket, to make it seem cheap, anyway,' she retorted. 'I just found a young man doing something to a horse's leg with a sponge and pail. And I held out one sovereign, and I said, "Do you know what this is?" He said, "No," and he'd call his father. And the old man came, and he said it was a spade guinea; and he said was it my own to do as I liked with, and I said "Yes"; and I asked about the pony-cart, and I said he could have the guinea if he'd drive us into Rochester. And his name is S. Crispin. And he said, "Right oh." '

It was a new sensation to be driven in a smart pony-trap along pretty country roads; it was very pleasant too (which is not always the case with new sensations), quite apart from the beautiful plans of spending the money which each child made as they went along, silently of course and quite to itself, for they felt it would never have done to let the old innkeeper hear them talk in the affluent sort of way they were thinking in. The old man put them down by the bridge at their request.

'If you were going to buy a carriage and horses, where would you go?' asked Cyril, as if he were only asking for the sake of something to say.

'Billy Peasmarsh, at the Saracen's Head,' said the old man promptly. 'Though all forbid I should recommend any man where it's a question of horses, no more than I'd take anybody else's recommending if I was a-buying one. But if your pa's thinking of a turnout of any sort, there ain't a straighter man in Rochester, nor a civiller spoken, than Billy, though I says it.'

'Thank you,' said Cyril. 'The Saracen's Head.'

And now the children began to see one of the laws of nature turn upside down and stand on its head like an acrobat. Any grown-up person would tell you that money is hard to get and easy to spend. But the fairy money had been easy to get, and spending it was not only hard, it was almost impossible. The tradespeople of Rochester seemed to shrink, to a trades-person, from the glittering fairy gold ('furrin money' they called it, for the most part). To begin with, Anthea, who had had the misfortune to sit on her hat earlier in the day, wished to buy another. She chose a very beautiful one, trimmed with pink roses and the blue breasts of peacocks. It was marked in the window, 'Paris Model, three guineas'.

'I'm glad,' she said, 'because, if it says guineas, it means guineas, and not sovereigns, which we haven't got.'

But when she took three of the spade guineas in her hand, which was by this time rather dirty owing to her not having put on gloves before going to the gravel-pit, the black-silk young lady in the shop looked very hard at her, and went and whispered something to an older and uglier lady, also in black silk, and then they gave her back the money and said it was not current coin.

'It's good money,' said Anthea, 'and it's my own.'

'I daresay,' said the lady, 'but it's not the kind of money that's fashionable now, and we don't care about taking it.'

'I believe they think we've stolen it,' said Anthea, rejoining the others in the street; 'if we had gloves they wouldn't think we were so dishonest. It's my hands being so dirty fills their minds with doubts.'

So they chose a humble shop, and the girls bought cotton gloves, the kind at sixpence three-farthings, but when they offered a guinea the woman looked at it through her spectacles and said she had no change; so the gloves had to be paid for out of Cyril's two-and-sevenpence that he meant to buy rabbits with, and so had the green imitation crocodile-skin purse at ninepence-halfpenny which had been bought at the same time. They tried several more shops, the kinds where you buy toys and scent, and silk handkerchiefs and books, and fancy boxes of stationery, and photographs of objects of interest in the vicinity. But nobody cared to change a guinea that day in Rochester, and as they went from shop to shop they got dirtier and dirtier, and their hair got more and more untidy, and Jane slipped and fell down on a part of the road where a water-cart had just gone by. Also they got very hungry, but they found no one would give them anything to eat for their guineas. After trying two pastrycooks in vain, they became so hungry, perhaps from the smell of the cake in the shops, as Cyril suggested, that they formed a plan of campaign in whispers and carried it out in desperation. They marched into a third pastrycook's – Beale, his name was – and before the people behind the counter could interfere each child had seized three new penny buns, clapped the three together between its dirty hands, and taken a big bite out of the triple sandwich. Then they stood at bay, with the twelve buns in their hands and their mouths very full indeed. The shocked pastrycook bounded round the corner.

'Here,' said Cyril, speaking as distinctly as he could, and holding out the guinea he got ready before entering the shop, 'pay yourself out of that.'

Mr Beale snatched the coin, bit it, and put it in his pocket.

'Off you go,' he said, brief and stern like the man in the song.

'But the change?' said Anthea, who had a saving mind.

'Change!' said the man. 'I'll change you! Hout you goes; and you may think yourselves lucky I don't send for the police to find out where you got it!'

In the Castle Gardens the millionaires finished the buns, and though the curranty softness of these were delicious, and acted like a charm in raising the spirits of the party, yet even the stoutest heart quailed at the thought of venturing to sound out Mr Billy Peasmarsh at the Saracen's Head on the subject of a horse and carriage. The boys would have given up the idea, but Jane was always a hopeful child, and Anthea generally an obstinate one, and their earnestness prevailed.

The whole party, by this time indescribably dirty, therefore betook itself to the Saracen's Head. The yard-method of attack having been successful at The Chequers was tried again here. Mr Peasmarsh was in the yard, and Robert opened the business in these terms –

'They tell me you have a lot of horses and carriages to sell.' It had been agreed that Robert should be spokesman, because in books it is always the gentlemen who buy horses, and not ladies, and Cyril had had his go at the Blue Boar.

'They tell you true, young man,' said Mr Peasmarsh. He was a long lean man, with very blue eyes and a tight mouth and narrow lips.

'We should like to buy some, please,' said Robert politely.

'I daresay you would.'

'Will you show us a few, please? To choose from.'

'Who are you a-kidden of?' inquired Mr Billy Peasmarsh. 'Was you sent here of a message?'

'I tell you,' said Robert, 'we want to buy some horses and car-riages, and a man told us you were straight and civil spoken, but I shouldn't wonder if he was mistaken.'

'Upon my sacred!' said Mr Peasmarsh. 'Shall I trot the whole stable out for your Honour's worship to see? Or shall I send round to the Bishop's to see if he's a nag or two to dispose of?'

'Please do,' said Robert, 'if it's not too much trouble. It would be very kind of you.'

Mr Peasmarsh put his hands in his pockets and laughed, and they did not like the way he did it. Then he shouted 'Willum!'

A stooping ostler appeared in a stable door.

'Here, Willum, come and look at this 'ere young dook! Wants to buy the whole stud, lock, stock, and bar'l. And ain't got tup-pence in his pocket to bless hisself with, I'll go bail!'

Willum's eyes followed his master's pointing thumb with con-temptuous interest.

'Do 'e, for sure?' he said.

But Robert spoke, though both the girls were now pulling at his jacket and begging him to 'come along'. He spoke, and he was very angry; he said:

'I'm not a young duke, and I never pretended to be. And as for tuppence – what do you call this?' And before the others could stop him he had pulled out two fat handfuls of shining guineas, and held them out for Mr Peasmarsh to look at. He did look. He snatched one up in his finger and thumb. He bit it, and Jane expected him to say, 'The best horse in my stables is at your service.' But the others knew better. Still it was a blow, even to the most desponding, when he said shortly:

'Willum, shut the yard doors,' and Willum grinned and went to shut them.

'Good-afternoon,' said Robert hastily; 'we shan't buy any of your horses now, whatever you say, and I hope it'll be a lesson to you.' He had seen a little side gate open, and was moving towards it as he spoke. But Billy Peasmarsh put himself in the way.

'Not so fast, you young off-scouring!' he said. 'Willum, fetch the pleece.'

Willum went. The children stood huddled together like frightened sheep, and Mr Peasmarsh spoke to them till the pleece arrived. He said many things. Among other things he said:

'Nice lot you are, aren't you, coming tempting honest men with your guineas!'

'They *are* guineas,' said Cyril boldly.

'Oh, of course we don't know all about that, no more we don't – oh no – course not! And dragging little gells into it, too. 'Ere – I'll let the gells go if you'll come along to the pleece quiet.'

'We won't be let go,' said Jane heroically; 'not without the boys. It's our money just as much as theirs, you wicked old man.'

'Where'd you get it, then?' said the man, softening slightly, which was not at all what the boys expected when Jane began to call him names.

Jane cast a silent glance of agony at the others.

'Lost your tongue, eh? Got it fast enough when it's for calling names with. Come, speak up. Where'd you get it?'

'Out of the gravel-pit,' said truthful Jane.

'Next article,' said the man.

'I tell you we did,' Jane said. 'There's a fairy there – all over brown fur – with ears like a bat's and eyes like a snail's, and he gives you a wish a day, and they all come true.'

'Touched in the head, eh?' said the man in a low voice, 'all the more shame to you boys dragging the poor afflicted child into your sinful burglaries.'

'She's not mad; it's true,' said Anthea; 'there is a fairy. If I ever see him again I'll wish for something for you; at least I would if vengeance wasn't wicked – so there!'

'Lor' lumme,' said Billy Peasmarsh, 'if there ain't another of 'em!'

And now Willum came back, with a spiteful grin on his face, and at his back a policeman, with whom Mr Peasmarsh spoke long in a hoarse earnest whisper.

'I daresay you're right,' said the policeman at last. 'Anyway, I'll take 'em up on a charge of unlawful possession, pending inquiries. And the magistrate will deal with the case. Send the afflicted ones to a home, as likely as not, and the boys to a reformatory. Now then, come along, youngsters! No use making a fuss. You bring the gells along, Mr Peasmarsh, sir, and I'll shepherd the boys.'

Speechless with rage and horror, the four children were driven along the streets of Rochester. Tears of anger and shame blinded them, so that when Robert ran right into a passer-by he did not recognise her till a well-known voice said, 'Well, if ever I did. Oh, Master Robert, whatever have you been a-doing of now?' And another voice, quite as well known, said, 'Panty; want go own Panty!'

They had run into Martha and the baby!

Martha behaved admirably. She refused to believe a word of the policeman's story, or of Mr Peasmarsh's either, even when they made Robert turn out his pockets in an archway and show the guineas.

'I don't see nothing,' she said. 'You've gone out of your senses, you two! There ain't any gold there – only the poor child's hands, all over crock and dirt, and like the very chimbley. Oh that I should ever see the day!'

And the children thought this very noble of Martha, even if rather wicked, till they remembered how the Fairy had promised that the servants should never notice any of the fairy gifts. So of course Martha couldn't see the gold, and so was only speaking the truth, and that was quite right, of course, but not extra noble.

It was getting dusk when they reached the police-station. The policeman told his tale to an inspector, who sat in a large bare room with a thing like a clumsy nursery-fender at one end to put prisoners in. Robert wondered whether it was a cell or a dock.

'Produce the coins, officer,' said the inspector.

'Turn out your pockets,' said the constable.

Cyril desperately plunged his hands in his pockets, stood still a moment, and then began to laugh – an odd sort of laugh that hurt, and that felt much more like crying. His pockets were empty. So were the pockets of the others. For of course at sunset all the fairy gold had vanished away.

'Turn out your pockets, and stop that noise,' said the inspector.

Cyril turned out his pockets, every one of the nine which enriched his Norfolk suit. And every pocket was empty.

'Well!' said the inspector.

'I don't know how they done it – artful little beggars! They walked in front of me the 'ole way, so as for me to keep my eye on them and not to attract a crowd and obstruct the traffic.'

'It's very remarkable,' said the inspector, frowning.

'If you've quite done a-browbeating of the innocent children,' said Martha, 'I'll hire a private carriage and we'll drive home to their papa's mansion. You'll hear about this again, young man! – I told you they hadn't got any gold, when you were pretending to see it in their poor helpless hands. It's early in the day for a constable on duty not to be able to trust his own eyes. As to the other one, the less said the better; he keeps the Saracen's Head, and he knows best what his liquor's like.'

'Take them away, for goodness' sake,' said the inspector crossly. But as they left the police-station he said, 'Now then!' to the policeman and Mr Peasmarsh, and he said it twenty times as crossly as he had spoken to Martha.

· · ·

Martha was as good as her word. She took them home in a very grand carriage, because the carrier's cart was gone, and, though she had stood by them so nobly with the police, she was so angry with them as soon as they were alone for 'trespassing into Rochester by themselves,' that none of them dared to mention the old man with the pony-cart from the village who was waiting for them in Rochester. And so, after one day of boundless wealth, the children found themselves sent to bed in deep disgrace, and only enriched by two pairs of cotton gloves, dirty inside because of the state of the hands they had been put on to cover, an imitation crocodile-skin purse, and twelve penny buns, long since digested.

The thing that troubled them most was the fear that the old gentleman's guinea might have disappeared at sunset with all the rest, so they went down to the village the next day to apologise for not meeting him in Rochester, and to *see*. They found him very friendly. The guinea had *not* disappeared, and he had bored a hole in it and hung it on his watch-chain. As for the guinea the baker took, the children felt they *could* not care whether it had vanished or not, which was not perhaps very honest, but on the other hand was not wholly unnatural. But afterwards this preyed on Anthea's mind, and at last she secretly sent twelve stamps by post to 'Mr Beale, Baker, Rochester.' Inside she wrote, 'To pay for the buns.' I hope the guinea did disappear, for that pastrycook was really not at all a nice man, and, besides, penny buns are seven for sixpence in all really respectable shops.

Chapter III

BEING WANTED

The morning after the children had been in possession of boundless wealth, and had been unable to buy anything really useful or enjoyable with it, except two pairs of cotton gloves, twelve penny buns, an imitation crocodile-skin purse, and a ride in a pony-cart, they awoke without any of the enthusiastic happiness which they had felt on the previous day when they remembered how they had had the luck to find a Psammead, or Sand-fairy, and to receive its promise to grant them a new wish every day. For now they had had two wishes, Beauty and Wealth, and neither had exactly made them happy. But the happening of strange things, even if they are not completely pleasant things, is more amusing than those times when nothing happens but meals, and they are not always completely pleasant, especially on the days when it is cold mutton or hash.

There was no chance of talking things over before breakfast, because everyone overslept itself, as it happened, and it needed a

vigorous and determined struggle to get dressed so as to be only
ten minutes late for breakfast. During this meal some efforts were
made to deal with the question of the Psammead in an impartial
spirit, but it is very difficult to discuss anything thoroughly and at
the same time to attend faithfully to your baby brother's breakfast
needs. The Baby was particularly lively that morning. He not only
wriggled his body through the bar of his high chair, and hung by
his head, choking and purple, but he collared a tablespoon with
desperate suddenness, hit Cyril heavily on the head with it, and
then cried because it was taken away from him. He put his fist in
his bread-and-milk, and demanded 'nam', which was only allowed
for tea. He sang, he put his feet on the table – he clamoured to 'go
walky'. The conversation was something like this:

'Look here – about that Sandy-fairy – Look out! – he'll have the
milk over.'

Milk removed to a safe distance.

'Yes – about that Fairy – No, Lamb dear, give Panther the narky
poon.'

Then Cyril tried. 'Nothing we've had yet has turned out – He
nearly had the mustard that time!'

'I wonder whether we'd better wish – Hullo! – you've done it
now, my boy!' And, in a flash of glass and pink baby-paws, the
bowl of golden carp in the middle of the table rolled on its side and
poured a flood of mixed water and goldfish into the Baby's lap and
into the laps of the others.

Everyone was almost as much upset as the goldfish; the Lamb
only remaining calm. When the pool on the floor had been

mopped up, and the leaping, gasping goldfish had been collected and put back in the water, the Baby was taken away to be entirely redressed by Martha, and most of the others had to change completely. The pinafores and jackets that had been bathed in goldfish-and-water were hung out to dry, and then it turned out that Jane must either mend the dress she had torn the day before or appear all day in her best petticoat. It was white and soft and frilly, and trimmed with lace, and very, very pretty, quite as pretty as a frock, if not more so. Only it was *not* a frock, and Martha's word was law. She wouldn't let Jane wear her best frock, and she refused to listen for a moment to Robert's suggestion that Jane should wear her best petticoat and call it a dress.

'It's not respectable,' she said. And when people say that, it's no use anyone's saying anything. You will find this out for yourselves some day.

So there was nothing for it but for Jane to mend her frock. The hole had been torn the day before when she happened to tumble down in the High Street of Rochester, just where a water-cart had passed on its silvery way. She had grazed her knee, and her stocking was much more than grazed, and her dress was cut by the same stone which had attended to the knees and the stocking. Of course the others were not such sneaks as to abandon a comrade in misfortune, so they all sat on the grass-plot round the sundial, and Jane darned away for dear life. The Lamb was still in the hands of Martha having its clothes changes, so conversation was possible.

Anthea and Robert timidly tried to conceal their inmost

thought, which was that the Psammead was not to be trusted; but Cyril said:

'Speak out – say what you've got to say – I hate hinting, and "don't know", and sneakish ways like that.'

So then Robert said, as in honour bound: 'Sneak yourself – Anthea and me weren't so goldfishy as you two were, so we got changed quicker, and we've had time to think it over, and if you ask me –'

'I didn't ask you,' said Jane, biting off a needleful of thread as she had always been strictly forbidden to do.

'I don't care who asks or who doesn't,' said Robert, 'but Anthea and I think the Sammyadd is a spiteful brute. If it can give us our wishes I suppose it can give itself its own, and I feel almost sure it wishes every time that our wishes shan't do us any good. Let's let the tiresome beast alone, and just go and have a jolly good game of forts, on our own, in the chalk-pit.'

(You will remember that the happily situated house where these children were spending their holidays lay between a chalk-quarry and a gravel-pit.)

Cyril and Jane were more hopeful – they generally were.

'I don't think the Sammyadd does it on purpose,' Cyril said; 'and, after all, it *was* silly to wish for boundless wealth. Fifty pounds in two-shilling pieces would have been much more sensible. And wishing to be beautiful as the day was simply donkeyish. I don't want to be disagreeable, but it *was*. We must try to find a really useful wish, and wish it.'

Jane dropped her work and said:

'I think so too, it's too silly to have a chance like this and not use it. I never heard of anyone else outside a book who had such a chance; there must be simply heaps of things we could wish for that wouldn't turn out Dead Sea fish, like these two things have. Do let's think hard, and wish something nice, so that we can have a real jolly day – what there is left of it.'

Jane darned away again like mad, for time was indeed getting on, and everyone began to talk at once. If you had been there you could not possibly have made head or tail of the talk, but these children were used to talking 'by fours,' as soldiers march, and each of them could say what it had to say quite comfortably, and listen to the agreeable sound of its own voice, and at the same time have three-quarters of two sharp ears to spare for listening to what the others said. That is an easy example in multiplication of vulgar fractions, but, as I daresay you can't do even that, I won't ask you to tell me whether $\frac{3}{4} \times 2 = 1\frac{1}{2}$, but I will ask you to believe me that this was the amount of ear each child was able to lend to the others. Lending ears was common in Roman times, as we learn from Shakespeare; but I fear I am getting too instructive.

When the frock was darned, the start for the gravel-pit was delayed by Martha's insisting on everybody's washing its hands – which was nonsense, because nobody had been doing anything at all, except Jane, and how can you get dirty doing nothing? That is a difficult question, and I cannot answer it on paper. In real life I could very show you – or you me, which is much more likely.

During the conversation in which the six ears were lent (there were four children, so *that* sum comes right), it had been decided that fifty pounds in two-shilling pieces was the right wish to have. And the lucky children, who could have anything in the wide world by just wishing for it, hurriedly started for the gravel- pit to express their wishes to the Psammead. Martha caught them at the gate, and insisted on their taking the Baby with them.

'Not want him indeed! Why, everybody 'ud want him, a duck! with all their hearts they would! and you know you promised your ma to take him out every blessed day,' said Martha.

'I know we did,' said Robert in gloom, 'but I wish the Lamb wasn't quite so young and small. It would be much better fun taking him out.'

'He'll mend of his youngness with time,' said Martha; 'and for his smallness, I don't think you'd fancy carrying of him any more, however big he was. Besides he can walk a bit, bless his precious fat legs, a ducky! He feels the benefit of the new-laid air, so he does, a pet!'

With this and a kiss, she plumped the Lamb into Anthea's arms, and went back to make new pinafores on the sewing-machine. She was a rapid performer on this instrument.

The Lamb laughed with pleasure, and said, 'Walky wif Panty,' and rode on Robert's back with yells of joy, and tried to feed Jane with stones, and altogether made himself so agreeable that nobody could long be sorry that he was of the party.

The enthusiastic Jane even suggested that they should devote a week's wishes to assuring the Baby's future, by asking such gifts for him as the good fairies give to Infant Princes in proper fairy-tales, but Anthea soberly reminded her that as the Sand-fairy's wishes only lasted till sunset they could not ensure any benefit to the Baby's later years; and Jane owned that it would be better to wish for fifty pounds in two-shilling pieces, and buy the Lamb a three-pound-fifteen rocking-horse, like those in the Army and Navy Stores list, with part of the money.

It was settled that, as soon as they had wished for the money and got it, they would get Mr Crispin to drive them into Rochester again, taking Martha with them if they could not get out of taking her. And they would make a list of the things they really wanted before they started. Full of high hopes and excellent resolutions, they went round the safe slow cart-road to the gravel-pits, and as they went in between the mounds of gravel a sudden thought came to them, and would have turned their ruddy cheeks pale if they had been children in a book. Being real live children, it only made them stop and look at each other with rather blank and silly expressions. For now they remembered that yesterday, when they had asked the Psammead for boundless wealth, and it was getting ready to fill the quarry with the minted gold of bright guineas – millions of them – it had told the children to run along outside the quarry for fear they should be buried alive in the heavy splendid treasure. And they had run. And so it happened that they had not had time to mark the spot where the Psammead was with a ring of stones, as before. And it was this thought that put such silly expressions on their faces.

'Never mind,' said the hopeful Jane, 'we'll soon find him.'

But this, though easily said, was hard in the doing. They looked and they looked, and though they found their seaside spades, nowhere could they find the Sand-fairy.

At last they had to sit down and rest – not at all because they were weary or disheartened, of course, but because the Lamb insisted on being put down, and you cannot look very carefully after anything you may have happened to lose in the sand if you have an active baby to look after at the same time. Get someone to drop your best knife in the sand next time you go to the seaside, and then take your baby brother with you when you go to look for it, and you will see that I am right.

The Lamb, as Martha had said, was feeling the benefit of the country air and he was as frisky as a sandhopper. The elder ones longed to go on talking about the new wishes they would have when (or if) they found the Psammead again. But the Lamb wished to enjoy himself.

He watched his opportunity and threw a handful of sand into Anthea's face, and then suddenly burrowed his own head in the sand and waved his fat legs in the air. Then of course the sand got into his eyes as it had into Anthea's, and he howled.

The thoughful Robert had brought one solid brown bottle of ginger-beer with him, relying on a thirst that had never yet failed him. This had to be uncorked hurriedly – it was the only wet thing within reach, and it was necessary to wash the sand out of the Lamb's eyes somehow. Of course the ginger hurt horribly, and he howled more than ever. And, amid his anguish of kicking, the bottle was upset and the beautiful ginger-beer frothed out into the sand and was lost for ever.

It was then that Robert, usually a very patient brother, so far forgot himself as to say:

'Anybody would want him, indeed! Only they don't; Martha doesn't, not really, or she'd jolly well keep him with her. He's a little nuisance, that's what he is. It's too bad. I only wish everybody *did* want him with all their hearts; we might get some peace in our lives.'

The Lamb stopped howling now, because Jane had suddenly remembered that there is only one safe way of taking things out of little children's eyes, and that is with your own soft wet tongue. It is quite easy if you love the Baby as much as you ought to.

Then there was a little silence. Robert was not proud of himself for having been so cross, and the others were not proud of him either. You often notice that sort of silence when someone has said something it ought not to – and everyone else holds its tongue and waits for the one who oughtn't to have said it is sorry.

The silence was broken by a sigh – a breath suddenly let out. The children's heads turned as if there had been a string tied to each nose, and someone had pulled all the strings at once.

And everyone saw the Sand-fairy sitting quite close to them, with the expression it used as a smile on its hairy face.

'Good-morning,' it said; 'I did that quite easily! Everyone wants him now.'

'It doesn't matter,' said Robert sulkily, because he knew he had been behaving rather like a pig. 'No matter who wants him – there's no one here to – anyhow.'

'Ingratitude,' said the Psammead, 'is a dreadful vice.'

'We're not ungrateful,' Jane made haste to say, 'but we didn't *really* want that wish. Robert only just said it. Can't you take it back and give us a new one?'

'No – I can't,' the Sand-fairy said shortly; 'chopping and changing – it's not business. You ought to be careful what you *do* wish. There was a little boy once, he'd wished for a Plesiosaurus instead of an Ichthyosaurus, because he was too lazy to remember the easy names of everyday things, and his father had been very vexed with him, and had made him go to bed before tea-time, and wouldn't let him go out in the nice flint boat along with the other children – it was the annual school-treat next day – and he came and flung himself down near me on the morning of the treat, and he kicked his little prehistoric legs about and said he wished he was dead. And of course then he was.'

'How awful!' said the children all together.

'Only till sunset, of course,' the Psammead said; 'still it was quite enough for his father and mother. And he caught it when he woke up – I can tell you. He didn't turn to stone – I forget why – but there must have been some reason. They didn't know being dead is only being asleep, and you're bound to wake up somewhere or other, either where you go to sleep or in some better place. You may be sure he caught it, giving them such a turn. Why, he wasn't allowed to taste Megatherium for a month after that. Nothing but oysters and periwinkles, and common things like that.'

All the children were quite crushed by this terrible tale. They looked at the Psammead in horror. Suddenly the Lamb perceived that something brown and furry was near him.

'Poof, poof, poofy,' he said, and made a grab.

'It's not a pussy,' Anthea was beginning, when the Sand-fairy leaped back.

'Oh, my left whisker!' it said; 'don't let him touch me. He's wet.'

Its fur stood on end with horror – and indeed a good deal of the ginger-beer had been spilt on the blue smock of the Lamb.

The Psammead dug with its hands and feet, and vanished in an instant and a whirl of sand.

The children marked the spot with a ring of stones.

'We may as well get along home,' said Robert. 'I'll say I'm sorry; but anyway if it's no good it's no harm, and we know where the sandy thing is for tomorrow.'

The others were noble. No one reproached Robert at all. Cyril picked up the Lamb, who was now quite himself again, and off they went by the safe cart-road.

The cart-road from the gravel-pits joins the road almost directly.

At the gate into the road the party stopped to shift the Lamb from Cyril's back to Robert's. And as they paused a very smart open carriage came in sight, with a coachman and a groom on the box, and inside the carriage a lady – very grand indeed, with a dress all white lace and red ribbons and a parasol all red and white – and a white fluffy dog on her lap with a red ribbon round its neck. She looked at the children, and particularly at the Baby, and she smiled at him. The children were used to this, for the Lamb was, as all the servants said, a 'very taking child'. So they

Mr. Beale snatched the coin and bit it

Down the dusty road went the smart carriage

He snatched the baby from Anthea

She swooped down towards the terror-stricken grower of plums, and slipped the coin into the pocket of his jacket . . .

waved their hands politely to the lady and expected her to drive on. But she did not. Instead she made the coachman stop. And she beckoned to Cyril, and when he went up to the carriage she said:

'What a dear darling duck of a baby! Oh, I *should* so like to adopt it! Do you think its mother would mind?'

'She'd mind very much indeed,' said Anthea shortly.

'Oh, but I should bring it up in luxury, you know. I am Lady Chittenden. You must have seen my photograph in the illustrated papers. They call me a beauty, you know, but of course that's all nonsense. Anyway –'

She opened the carriage door and jumped out. She had the wonderfullest red high-heeled shoes with silver buckles. 'Let me hold him a minute,' she said. And she took the Lamb and held him very awkwardly, as if she was not used to babies.

Then suddenly she jumped into the carriage with the Lamb in her arms and slammed the door and said, 'Drive on!'

The Lamb roared, the little white dog barked, and the coachman hesitated.

'Drive on, I tell you!' cried the lady; and the coachman did, for, as he said afterwards, it was as much as his place was worth not to.

The four children looked at each other, and then with one accord they rushed after the carriage and held on behind. Down the dusty road went the smart carriage, and after it, at double-quick time, ran the twinkling legs of the Lamb's brothers and sisters.

The Lamb howled louder and louder, but presently his howls

changed by slow degrees to hiccupy gurgles, and then all was still and they knew he had gone to sleep.

The carriage went on, and the eight feet that twinkled through the dust were growing quite stiff and tired before the carriage stopped at the lodge of a grand park. The children crouched down behind the carriage, and the lady got out. She looked at the Baby as it lay on the carriage seat, and hesitated.

'The darling – I won't disturb it,' she said, and went into the lodge to talk to the woman there about a setting of Buff Orpington eggs that had not turned out well.

The coachman and footman sprang from the box and bent over the sleeping Lamb.

'Fine boy – wish he was mine,' said the coachman.

'He wouldn't favour *you* much,' said the groom sourly; 'too 'andsome.'

The coachman pretended not to hear. He said:

'Wonder at her now – I do really! Hates kids. Got none of her own, and can't abide other folkses'.'

The children, crouching in the white dust under the carriage, exchanged uncomfortable glances.

'Tell you what,' the coachman went on firmly, 'blowed if I don't hide the little nipper in the hedge and tell her his brothers took 'im! Then I'll come back for him afterwards.'

'No, you don't,' said the footman. 'I've took to that kid so as never was. If anyone's to have him, it's me – so there!'

'Stow your gab!' the coachmen rejoined. 'You don't want no kids, and, if you did, one kid's the same as another to you. But I'm a married man and a judge of breed. I knows a first-rate yearling when I sees him. I'm a-goin' to 'ave him, an' least said soonest mended.'

'I should 'a' thought,' said the footman sneeringly, 'you'd a'most enough. What with Alfred, an' Albert, an' Louise, an' Victor Stanley, an' Helena Beatrice, an' another –'

The coachman hit the footman in the chin – the footman hit the coachman in the waistcoat – the next minute the two were fighting here and there, in and out, up and down, and all over everywhere, and the little dog jumped on the box of the carriage and began barking like mad.

Cyril, still crouching in the dust, waddled on bent legs to the side of the carriage farthest from the battlefield. He unfastened the door of the carriage – the two men were far too much occupied with their quarrel to notice anything – took the Lamb in his arms, and, still stooping, carried the sleeping baby a dozen yards along the road to where a stile led into a wood. The others followed, and there among the hazels and young oaks and sweet chestnuts, covered by high strong-scented bracken, they all lay hidden till the angry voices of the men were hushed at the angry voice of the red-and-white lady, and, after a long and anxious search, the carriage at last drove away.

'My only hat!' said Cyril, drawing a deep breath as the sound of wheels at last died away. 'Everyone *does* want him now – and no mistake! That Sammyadd has done us again! Tricky brute! For any sake, let's get the kid safe home.'

So they peeped out, and finding on the right-hand only lonely white road, and nothing but lonely white road on the left, they took courage, and the road, Anthea carrying the sleeping Lamb.

Adventures dogged their footsteps. A boy with a bundle of faggots on his back dropped his bundle by the roadside and asked to look at the Baby, and then offered to carry him; but Anthea was not to be caught that way twice. They all walked on, but the boy followed, and Cyril and Robert couldn't make him go away till they had more than once invited him to smell their fists. Afterwards a little girl in a blue-and-white checked pinafore actually followed them for a quarter of a mile crying for 'the precious Baby,' and then she was only got rid of by threats of tying her to a tree in the wood with all their pocket-handkerchiefs. 'So that the bears can come and eat you as soon as it gets dark,' said Cyril severely. Then she went off crying. It presently seemed wise, to the brothers and sisters of the Baby, who was wanted by everyone, to hide in the hedge whenever they saw anyone coming, and thus they managed to prevent the Lamb from arousing the inconvenient affection of a milkman, a stone-breaker, and a man who drove a cart with a paraffin barrel at the back of it. They were nearly home when the worst thing of all happened. Turning a corner suddenly they came upon two vans, a tent, and a company of gipsies encamped by the side of the road. The vans were hung all round with wicker chairs and cradles, and flower-stands and feather brushes. A lot of ragged children were industriously making dust-pies in the road, two men lay on the grass smoking, and three women were doing the family washing in an old red watering-can with the top broken off.

In a moment every gipsy, men, women, and children, sur-rounded Anthea and the Baby.

'Let *me* hold him, little lady,' said one of the gipsy women, who had a mahogany-coloured face and dust-coloured hair; 'I won't hurt a hair of his head, the little picture!'

'I'd rather not,' said Anthea.

'Let me have him,' said the other woman, whose face was also of the hue of mahogany, and her hair jet-black, in greasy curls. 'I've nineteen of my own, so I have.'

'No,' said Anthea bravely, but her heart beat fast so that it nearly choked her.

Then one of the men pushed forward.

'Swelp me if it ain't!' he cried, 'my own long-lost child! Have he a strawberry mark on his left ear? No? Then he's my own baby, stolen from me in hinnocent hinfancy. 'And 'im over – and we'll not 'ave the law on yer this time.'

He snatched the Baby from Anthea, who turned scarlet and burst into tears of pure rage.

The others were standing quite still; this was much the most ter-rible thing that had ever happened to them. Even being taken up by the police in Rochester was nothing to this. Cyril was quite white, and his hands trembled a little, but he made a sign to the others to shut up. He was silent a minute, thinking hard. Then he said:

'We don't want to keep him if he's yours. But you see he's used to us. You shall have him if you want him.'

'No, no!' cried Anthea – and Cyril glared at her.

'Of course we want him,' said the woman, trying to get the Baby out of the man's arms. The Lamb howled loudly.

'Oh, he's hurt!' shrieked Anthea; and Cyril, in a savage undertone, bade her 'Stow it!'

'You trust to me,' he whispered. 'Look here,' he went on, 'he's awfully tiresome with people he doesn't know very well. Suppose we stay here a bit till he gets used to you, and then when it's bedtime I give you my word of honour we'll go away and let you keep him if you want to. And then when we're gone you can decide which of you is to have him, as you all want him so much.'

'That's fair enough,' said the man who was holding the Baby, trying to loosen the red neckerchief which the Lamb had caught hold of and drawn round his mahogany throat so tight that he could hardly breathe. The gipsies whispered together, and Cyril took the chance to whisper too. He said, 'Sunset! we'll get away then.'

And then his brother and sisters were filled with wonder and admiration at his having been so clever as to remember this.

'Oh, do let him come to us,' said Jane. 'See, we'll sit down here and take care of him for you till he gets used to you.'

'What about dinner?' said Robert suddenly. The others looked at him with scorn. 'Fancy bothering about your beastly dinner when your br – I mean when the Baby –' Jane whispered hotly. Robert carefully winked at her and went on:

'You won't mind my just running home to get our dinner?' he said to the gipsies; 'I can bring it out here in a basket.'

His brother and sisters felt themselves very noble, and despised him. They did not know his thoughtful secret intention. But the gipsies did in a minute.

'Oh yes!' they said; 'and then fetch the police with a pack of lies about it being your baby instead of ours! D'jever catch a weasel asleep?' they asked.

'If you're hungry you can pick a bit along of us,' said the light-haired gipsy woman, not unkindly. 'Here, Levi, that blessed kid'll howl all his buttons off. Give him to the little lady, and let's see if they can't get him used to us a bit.'

So the Lamb was handed back; but the gipies crowded so closely that he could not possibly stop howling. Then the man with the red neckerchief said:

'Here, Pharaoh, make up the fire; and you girls see to the pot. Give the kid a chanst.' So the gipsies, very much against their will, went off to their work, and the children and the Lamb were left sitting on the grass.

'He'll be all right at sunset,' Jane whispered. 'But, oh, it is awful! Suppose they are frightfully angry when they come to their senses! They might beat us, or leave us tied to trees, or something.'

'No, they won't,' Anthea said. ('O, my Lamb, don't cry any more, it's all right, Panty's got oo, duckie!') 'They aren't unkind people, or they wouldn't be going to give us any dinner.'

'Dinner?' said Robert. 'I won't touch their nasty dinner. It would choke me!'

The others thought so too then. But when the dinner was ready – it turned out to be supper, and happened between four and five – they were all glad enough to take what they could get. It was boiled rabbit, with onions, and some bird rather like a chicken, but stringier about the legs and with a stronger taste. The Lamb had bread soaked in hot water and brown sugar sprinkled on the top. He liked this very much, and consented to let the two gipsy women feed him with it, as he sat on Anthea's lap. All that long hot afternoon Robert and Cyril and Anthea and Jane had to keep the Lamb amused and happy, while the gipsies looked eagerly on. By the time the shadows grew long and black across the meadows he had really 'taken to' the woman with the light hair, and even consented to kiss his hand to the children, and to stand up and bow, with his hand on his chest – 'like a gentleman' – to the two men. The whole gipsy camp was in raptures with him, and his brothers and sisters could not help taking some pleasure in showing off his accomplishments to an audience so interested and enthusiastic. But they longed for sunset.

'We're getting into the habit of longing for sunset,' Cyril whispered. 'How I do wish we could wish something really sensible, that would be of some use, so that we should be quite sorry when sunset came.'

The shadows got longer and longer, and at last there were no separate shadows any more, but one soft glowing shadow over everything; for the sun was out of sight – behind the hill – but he had not really set yet. The people who make the laws about lighting bicycle lamps are the people who decide when the sun sets; he has to do it, too, to the minute, or they would know the reason why!

But the gipsies were getting impatient.

'Now, young uns,' the red-handkerchief man said, 'it's time you were laying of your heads on your pillows – so it is! The kid's all right and friendly with us now – so you just hand him over and sling that hook o' yours like you said.'

The women and children came crowding round the Lamb, arms were held out, fingers snapped invitingly, friendly faces beaming with admiring smiles; but all failed to tempt the loyal Lamb. He clung with arms and legs to Jane, who happened to be holding him, and uttered the gloomiest roar of the whole day.

'It's no good,' the woman said, 'hand the little poppet over, miss. We'll soon quiet him.'

And still the sun would not set.

'Tell her about how to put him to bed,' whispered Cyril; 'anything to gain time – and be ready to bolt when the sun really does make up its silly old mind to set.'

'Yes, I'll hand him over in just one minute,' Anthea began, talking very fast – 'but do let me just tell you he has a warm bath every night and cold in the morning, and he has a crockery rabbit to go into the warm bath with him, and little Samuel saying his prayers in white china on a red cushion for the cold bath; and he hates you to wash his ears, but you must; and if you let the soap get into his eyes, the Lamb –'

'Lamb kyes,' said he – he had stopped roaring to listen.

The woman laughed. 'As if I hadn't never bath'd a babby!' she said. 'Come – give us a hold of him. Come to 'Melia, my precious.'

'G'way, ugsie!' replied the Lamb at once.

'Yes, but,' Anthea went on, 'about his meals; you really *must* let me tell you he has an apple or a banana every morning, and bread-and-milk for breakfast, and an egg for his tea sometimes, and –'

'I've brought up ten,' said the black-ringleted woman, 'besides the others. Come, miss, 'and 'im over – I can't bear it no longer. I just must give him a hug.'

'We ain't settled yet whose he's to be, Esther,' said one of the men.

'It won't be you, Esther, with seven of 'em at your tail a'ready.'

'I ain't so sure of that,' said Esther's husband.

'And ain't I nobody, to have a say neither?' said the husband of 'Melia.

Zillah, the girl, said, 'An' me? I'm a single girl – and no one but 'im to look after – I ought to have him.'

'Hold your tongue!'

'Shut your mouth!'

'Don't you show me no more of your impudence!'

Everyone was getting very angry. The dark gipsy faces were frowning and anxious-looking. Suddenly a change swept over them, as if some invisible sponge had wiped away these cross and anxious expressions, and left only a blank.

The children saw that the sun really *had* set. But they were afraid to move. And the gipsies were feeling so muddled, because of the invisible sponge that had washed all the feelings of the last few hours out of their hearts, that they could not say a word.

The children hardly dared to breathe. Suppose the gipsies,

when they recovered speech, should be furious to think how silly they had been all day?

It was an awkward moment. Suddenly Anthea, greatly daring, held out the Lamb to the red-handkerchief man.

'Here he is!' she said.

The man drew back. 'I shouldn't like to deprive you, miss,' he said hoarsely.

'Anyone who likes can have my share of him,' said the other man.

'After all, I've got enough of my own,' said Esther.

'He's a nice little chap, though,' said Amelia. She was the only one who now looked affectionately at the whimpering Lamb.

Zillah said, 'If I don't think I must have had a touch of the sun. *I* don't want him.'

'Then shall we take him away?' said Anthea.

'Well, suppose you do,' said Pharaoh heartily, 'and we'll say no more about it!'

And with great haste all the gipsies began to be busy about their tents for the night. All but Amelia. She went with the children as far as the bend in the road – and there she said:

'Let me give him a kiss, miss – I don't know what made us go for to behave so silly. Us gipsies don't steal babies, whatever they may tell you when you're naughty. We've enough of our own, mostly. But I've lost all mine.'

She leaned towards the Lamb; and he, looking in her eyes, unexpectedly put up a grubby soft paw and stroked her face.

'Poor, poor!' said the Lamb. And he let the gipsy woman kiss him, and, what is more, he kissed her brown cheek in return – a very nice kiss, as all his kisses are, and not a wet one like some babies give. The gipsy woman moved her finger about on his forehead as if she had been writing something there, and the same with his chest and his hands and his feet; then she said:

'May he be brave, and have the strong head to think with, and the strong heart to love with, and the strong hands to work with, and the strong feet to travel with, and always come safe home to his own.' Then she said something in a strange language no one could understand, and suddenly added:

'Well, I must be saying "so long" – and glad to have made your acquaintance.' And she turned and went back to her home – the tent by the grassy roadside.

The children looked after her till she was out of sight. Then Robert said, 'How silly of her! Even sunset didn't put *her* right. What rot she talked!'

'Well,' said Cyril, 'if you ask me, I think it was rather decent of her –'

'Decent?' said Anthea; 'it was very nice indeed of her. I think she's a dear.'

'She's just too frightfully nice for anything,' said Jane.

And they went home – very late for tea and unspeakably late for dinner. Martha scolded, of course. But the Lamb was safe.

'I say – it turned out we wanted the Lamb as much as anyone,' said Robert later.

'Of course.'

'But do you feel different about it now the sun's set?'

'*No,*' said all the others together.

'Then it's lasted over sunset with us.'

'No, it hasn't,' Cyril explained. 'The wish didn't do anything to *us*. We always wanted him with all our hearts when we were our proper selves, only we were all pigs this morning; especially you, Robert.' Robert bore this much with a strange calm.

'I certainly *thought* I didn't want him this morning,' said he. 'Perhaps I was a pig. But everything looked so different when we thought we were going to lose him.'

Chapter IV

WINGS

The next day was very wet – too wet to go out, and far too wet to think of disturbing a Sand-fairy so sensitive to water that he still, after thousands of years, felt the pain of once having had his left whisker wetted. It was a long day, and it was not till the afternoon that all the children suddenly decided to write letters to their mother. It was Robert who had the misfortune to upset the ink-pot – an unusually deep and full one – straight into that part of Anthea's desk where she had long pretended that an arrangement of gum and cardboard painted with Indian ink was a secret drawer. It was not exactly Robert's fault; it was only his misfortune that he chanced to be lifting the ink across the desk just at the moment when Anthea had got it open, and that that same moment should have been the one chosen by the Lamb to get under the table and break his squeaking bird. There was a sharp convenient wire inside the bird, and of course the Lamb ran the wire into Robert's leg at once; and so, without anyone's meaning to, the secret drawer was flooded with ink. At the same time a stream was poured over Anthea's half-finished letter.

DARLING MOTHER,

I hope you are quite well, and I hope Granny is better.
The other day we . . .

Then came a flood of ink, and at the bottom these words in pencil –

It was not me upset the ink, but it took such a time clearing up, so no more as it is post-time. From your loving daughter,

ANTHEA.

Robert's letter had not even been begun. He had been drawing a ship on the blotting paper while he was trying to think of what to say. And of course after the ink was upset he had to help Anthea to clean out her desk, and he promised to make her another secret drawer, better than the other. And she said, 'Well, make it now.' So it was post-time and his letter wasn't done. And the secret drawer wasn't done either.

Cyril wrote a long letter, very fast, and then went to set a trap for slugs that he had read about in the *Home-made Gardener*, and when it was post-time the letter could not be found, and it never was found. Perhaps the slugs ate it.

Jane's letter was the only one that went. She meant to tell her mother all about the Psammead – in fact they had all meant to do this – but she spent so long thinking how to spell the word that there was no time to tell the story properly, and it is useless to tell a story unless you *do* tell it properly, so she had to be contented with this –

> My Dear Mother Dear,
>
> We are all as good as we can, like you told us to, and the Lamb has a little cold, but Martha says it is nothing, only he upset the goldfish into himself yesterday morning. When we were up at the sand-pit the other day we went round by the safe way where the carts go, and we found a –

Half an hour went by before Jane felt quite sure that they could none of them spell Psammead. And they could not find it in the dictionary either, though they looked. Then Jane hastily finished her letter:

> We found a strange thing, but it is nearly post-time, so no more at present from your little girl,
>
> Jane.
>
> P.S. If you could have a wish come true, what would you have?

Then the postman was heard blowing his horn, and Robert rushed out in the rain to stop his cart and give him the letters. And that was how it happened that, though all the children meant to tell their mother about the Sand-fairy, somehow or other she never got to know. There were other reasons why she never got to know, but these come later.

The next day Uncle Richard came and took them all to Maidstone in a waggonette – all except the Lamb. Uncle Richard was the very best kind of uncle. He bought them toys at Maidstone. He took them into a shop and let them choose exactly what they wanted, without any restrictions about price, and no nonsense about things being instructive. It is very wise to let children choose exactly what they like, because they are very foolish and inexperienced, and sometimes they will choose a really instructive thing without meaning to. This happened to Robert, who chose, at the last moment, and in a great hurry, a box with pictures on it of winged bulls with men's heads and winged men with eagles' heads. He thought there would be animals inside, the same as on the box. When he got it home it was a Sunday puzzle about ancient Nineveh. The others chose in haste, and were happy at leisure. Cyril had a model engine, and the girls had two dolls, as well as a china tea-set with forget-me-nots on it, to be 'between them'. The boys' 'between-them' was bow and arrows.

Then Uncle Richard took them on the beautiful Medway in a boat, and then they all had tea at a beautiful pastrycook's, and when they reached home it was far too late to have any wishes that day.

They did not tell Uncle Richard anything about the Psammead. I do not know why. And they do not know why. But I daresay you can guess.

The day after Uncle Richard had behaved so handsomely was a

very hot day indeed. The people who decide what the weather is to be, and put its orders down for it in the newspapers every morning, said afterwards that it was the hottest day there had been for years. They had ordered it to be 'warmer – some showers,' and warmer it certainly was. In fact it was so busy being warmer that it had no time to attend to the order about showers, so there weren't any.

Have you ever been up at five o'clock on a fine summer morning? It is very beautiful. The sunlight is pinky and yellowy, and all the grass and trees are covered with dew-diamonds. And all the shadows go the opposite way to the way they do in the evening, which is very interesting and makes you feel as though you were in a new other world.

Anthea awoke at five. She had made herself wake, and I must tell you how it is done, even if it keeps you waiting for the story to go on.

You get into bed at night, and lie down quite flat on your little back, with your hands straight down by your sides. Then you say 'I *must* wake up at five' (or six, or seven, or eight, or nine, whatever the time is that you want), and as you say it you push your chin down on to your chest and bang your head back on the pillow. And you do this as many times as there are ones in the time you want to wake up at. (It is quite an easy sum.) Of course everything depends on your really wanting to get up at five (or six, or seven, or eight, or nine); if you don't really want to, it's all of no use. But if you do – well, try it and see. Of course in this, as in doing Latin proses or getting into mischief, practice makes perfect.

Anthea was quite perfect.

At the very moment when she opened her eyes she heard the black-and-gold clock down in the dining-room strike eleven. So she knew it was three minutes to five. The black-and-gold clock always struck wrong, but it was all right when you knew what it meant. It was like a person talking a foreign language. If you know the language it is just as easy to understand as English. And Anthea knew the clock language. She was very sleepy, but she jumped out of bed and put her face and hands into a basin of cold water. This is a fairy charm that prevents you wanting to get back into bed again. Then she dressed, and folded up her nightgown. She did not tumble it together by the sleeves, but folded it by the seams from the hem, and that will show you the kind of well-brought-up little girl she was.

Then she took her shoes in her hand and crept softly down the stairs. She opened the dining-room window and climbed out. It would have been just as easy to go out by the door, but the window was more romantic, and less likely to be noticed by Martha.

'I will always get up at five,' she said to herself. 'It was quite too awfully pretty for anything.'

Her heart was beating very fast, for she was carrying out a plan quite her own. She could not be sure that it was a good plan, but she was quite sure that it would not be any better if she were to tell the others about it. And she had a feeling that, right or wrong, she would rather go through with it alone. She put on her shoes under the iron verandah, on the red-and-yellow shining tiles, and then she ran straight to the sand-pit, and found the Psammead's place, and dug it out; it was very cross indeed.

'It's too bad,' it said, fluffing up its fur like pigeons do their feathers at Christmas time. 'The weather's arctic, and it's the middle of the night.'

'I'm so sorry,' said Anthea gently, and she took off her white pinafore and covered the Sand-fairy up with it, all but its head, bat's ears, and its eyes that were like a snail's eyes.

'Thank you,' it said, 'that's better. What's the wish this morning?'

'I don't know,' said she; 'that's just it. You see, we've been very unlucky, so far. I wanted to talk to you about it. But – would you mind not giving me any wishes till after breakfast? It's so hard to talk to anyone if they jump out at you with wishes you don't really want!'

'You shouldn't say you wish for things if you don't wish for them. In the old days people almost always knew whether it was Megatherium or Ichthyosaurus they really wanted for dinner.'

'I'll try not,' said Anthea, 'but I do wish –'

'Look out!' said the Psammead in a warning voice, and it began to blow itself out.

'Oh, this isn't a magic wish – it's just – I should be so glad if you'd not swell yourself out and nearly burst to give me anything just now. Wait till the others are here.'

'Well, well,' it said indulgently, but it shivered.

'Would you,' asked Anthea kindly – 'would you like to come

and sit on my lap? You'd be warmer, and I could turn the skirt of my frock up round you. I'd be very careful.'

Anthea had never expected that it would, but it did.

'Thank you,' it said, 'you really are rather thoughtful.' It crept on to her lap and snuggled down, and she put her arms round with a rather frightened gentleness. 'Now then!' it said.

'Well then,' said Anthea, 'everything we have wished has turned out rather horrid. I wish you would advise us. You are so old, you must be very wise.'

'I was always generous from a child,' said the Sand-fairy. 'I've spent the whole of my waking hours in giving. But one thing I won't give – that's advice.'

'You see,' Anthea went on, 'it's such a wonderful thing – such a splendid, glorious chance. It's so good and kind and dear of you to give us our wishes, and it seems such a pity it should all be wasted just because we are too silly to know what to wish for.'

Anthea had meant to say that – and she had not wanted to say it before the others. It's one thing to say you're silly, and quite another to say that other people are.

'Child,' said the Sand-fairy sleepily, 'I can only advise you to think before you speak –'

'But I thought you never gave advice.'

'That piece doesn't count,' it said. 'You'll never take it! Besides, it's not original. It's in all the copy-books.'

'But won't you say if you think wings would be a silly wish?'

'Wings?' it said. 'I think you might do worse. Only, take care you aren't flying high at sunset. There was a little Ninevite boy I heard of once. He was one of King Sennacherib's sons, and a traveller brought him a Psammead. He used to keep it in a box of sand on the palace terrace. It was a dreadful degradation for one of us, of course; still, the boy *was* the Assyrian King's son. And one day he wished for wings and got them. But he forgot that they would turn into stone at sunset, and when they did he fell slap on to one of the winged lions at the top of his father's great staircase; and what with *his* stone wings and the lion's stone wings – well, it's not a pretty story! But I believe the boy enjoyed himself very much till then.'

'Tell me,' said Anthea, 'why don't our wishes turn into stone now? Why do they just vanish?'

'*Autre temps, autre mœurs,*' said the creature.

'Is that the Ninevite language?' asked Anthea, who had learned no foreign language at school except French.

'What I mean is,' the Psammead went on, 'that in the old days people wished for good solid everyday gifts – Mammoths and Pterodactyls and things – and those could be turned into stone as easy as not. But people wish such high-flying fanciful things nowadays. How are you going to turn being beautiful as the day, or being wanted by everybody, into stone? You see it can't be done. And it would never do to have two rules, so they simply vanish. If being beautiful as the day *could* be turned into stone it would last an awfully long time, you know – much longer than you would. Just look at the Greek statues. It's just as well as it is. Good-bye. I *am* so sleepy.'

It jumped off her lap – dug frantically, and vanished.

Anthea was late for breakfast. It was Robert who quietly poured a spoonful of treacle down the Lamb's frock, so that he had to be taken away and washed thoroughly directly after breakfast. And it was of course a very naughty thing to do; yet it served two purposes – it delighted the Lamb, who loved above all things to be completely sticky, and it engaged Martha's attention so that the others could slip away to the sand-pit without the Lamb.

They did it, and in the lane Anthea, breathless from the scurry of that slipping, panted out –

'I want to propose we take turns to wish. Only, nobody's to have a wish if the others don't think it's a nice wish. Do you agree?'

'Who's to have first wish?' asked Robert cautiously.

'Me, if you don't mind,' said Anthea apologetically. 'And I've thought about it – and it's wings.'

There was a silence. The others rather wanted to find fault, but it was hard, because the word 'wings' raised a flutter of joyous excitement in every breast.

'Not so dusty,' said Cyril generously; and Robert added, 'Really, Panther, you're not quite such a fool as you look.'

Jane said, 'I think it would be perfectly lovely. It's like a bright dream of delirium.'

They found the Sand-fairy easily. Anthea said:

'I wish we all had beautiful wings to fly with.'

The Sand-fairy blew himself out, and next moment each child felt a funny feeling, half heaviness and half lightness, on its shoulders. The Psammead put its head on one side and turned its snail's eyes from one to the other.

'Not so dusty,' it said dreamily. 'But really, Robert, you're not quite such an angel as you look.' Robert almost blushed.

The wings were very big, and more beautiful than you can possibly imagine – for they were soft and smooth, and every feather lay neatly in its place. And the feathers were of the most lovely mixed changing colours, like the rainbow, or iridescent glass, or the beautiful scum that sometimes floats on water that is not at all nice to drink.

'Oh – but can we fly?' Jane said, standing anxiously first on one foot and then on the other.

'Look out!' said Cyril; 'you're treading on my wing.'

'Does it hurt?' asked Anthea with interest; but no one answered, for Robert had spread his wings and jumped up, and now he was slowly rising in the air. He looked very awkward in his knickerbocker suit – his boots in particular hung helplessly, and seemed much larger than when he was standing in them. But the others cared but little how he looked – or how they looked, for that matter. For now they all spread out their wings and rose in the air. Of course you all know what flying feels like, because everyone has dreamed about flying, and it seems so beautifully easy – only, you can never remember how you did it; and as a rule you have to do it without wings, in your dreams, which is more clever and uncommon, but not so easy to remember the rule for. Now the four children rose flapping from the ground, and you can't think how good the air felt running against their faces. Their wings were tremendously wide when they were spread out, and they had to fly quite a long way apart so as not to get in each other's way. But little things like this are easily learned.

All the words in the English Dictionary, and in the Greek Lexicon as well, are, I find, of no use at all to tell you exactly what it feels like to be flying, so I will not try. But I will say that to look *down* on the fields and woods, instead of *along* at them, is something like looking at a beautiful live map, where, instead of silly colours on paper, you have real moving sunny woods and green fields laid out one after the other. As Cyril said, and I can't think where he got hold of such a strange expression, 'It does you a fair treat!' It was almost wonderful and more like real magic than any wish the children had had yet. They flapped and flew and sailed on their great rainbow wings, between green earth and blue sky; and they flew right over Rochester and then swerved round towards Maidstone, and presently they all began to feel extremely hungry. Curiously enough this happened when they were flying rather low, and just as they were crossing an orchard where some early plums shone red and ripe.

They paused on their wings. I cannot explain to you how this is done, but it is something like treading water when you are swimming, and hawks do it extremely well.

'Yes, I daresay,' said Cyril, though no one had spoken. 'But stealing is stealing even if you've got wings.'

'Do you really think so?' said Jane briskly. 'If you've got wings you're a bird, and no one minds birds breaking the commandments. At least, they may *mind*, but the birds always do it, and no one scolds them or sends them to prison.'

It was not so easy to perch on a plum-tree as you might think, because the rainbow wings were so *very* large; but somehow they all managed to do it, and the plums were certainly very sweet and juicy.

Fortunately, it was not till they had all had quite as many plums as were good for them that they saw a stout man, who looked exactly as though he owned the plum-trees, come hurrying through the orchard gate with a thick stick, and with one accord they disentangled their wings from the plum-laden branches and began to fly.

The man stopped short, with his mouth open. For he had seen the boughs of his trees moving and twitching, and he had said to himself, 'The young varmints – at it again!' And he had come out at once, for the lads of the village had taught him in past seasons that plums want looking after. But when he saw the rainbow wings flutter up out of the plum-tree he felt that he must have gone quite mad, and he did not like the feeling at all. And when Anthea looked down and saw his mouth go slowly open, and stay so, and his face become green and mauve in patches, she called out:

'Don't be frightened,' and felt hastily in her pocket for a three-penny-bit with a hole in it, which she had meant to hang on a ribbon round her neck, for luck. She hovered round the unfortunate plum-owner, and said; 'We have had some of your plums; we thought it wasn't stealing, but now I am not so sure. So here's some money to pay for them.'

She swooped down towards the terror-stricken grower of plums, and slipped the coin into the pocket of his jacket, and in a few flaps she had rejoined the others.

The farmer sat down on the grass, suddenly and heavily.

'Well – I'm blessed!' he said. 'This here is what they call delusions, I suppose. But this here threepenny' – he had pulled it out and bitten it, – '*that's* real enough. Well, from this day forth I'll be a better man. It's the kind of thing to sober a chap for life, this is. I'm glad it was only wings, though. I'd rather see birds as aren't there, and couldn't be, even if they pretend to talk, than some things as I could name.'

He got up slowly and heavily, and went indoors, and he was so nice to his wife that day that she felt quite happy, and said to herself, 'Law, whatever have a-come to the man!' and smartened herself up and put a blue ribbon bow at the place where her collar fastened on, and looked so pretty that he was kinder than ever. So perhaps the winged children really did do one good thing that day. If so, it was the only one; for really there is nothing like wings for getting you into trouble. But, on the other hand, if you are in trouble, there is nothing like wings for getting you out of it.

This was the case in the matter of the fierce dog who sprang out at them when they had folded up their wings as small as possible and were going up to a farm door to ask for a crust of bread and cheese, for in spite of the plums they were soon just as hungry as ever again.

Now there is no doubt whatever that, if the four had been

ordinary wingless children, that black and fierce dog would have had a good bite out of the brown-stockinged leg of Robert, who was the nearest. But at its first growl there was a flutter of wings, and the dog was left to strain at his chain and stand on his hind-legs as if he were trying to fly too.

They tried several other farms, but at those where there were no dogs the people were far too frightened to do anything but scream; and at last, when it was nearly four o'clock and their wings were getting miserably stiff and tired, they alighted on a church-tower and held a council of war.

'We can't possibly fly all the way home without dinner *or* tea,' said Robert with desperate decision.

'And nobody will give us any dinner, or even lunch, let alone tea,' said Cyril.

'Perhaps the clergyman here might,' suggested Anthea. 'He must know all about angels –'

'Anybody could see we're not that.' said Jane. 'Look at Robert's boot and Squirrel's plaid necktie.'

'Well,' said Cyril firmly, 'if the country you're in won't *sell* provisions, you *take* them. In wars I mean. I'm quite certain you do. And even in other stories no good brother would allow his little sister to starve in the midst of plenty.'

'Plenty?' repeated Robert hungrily; and the others looked vaguely round the bare leads of the church tower, and murmured, 'In the midst of?'

'Yes,' said Cyril impressively. 'There is a larder window at the side of the clergyman's house, and I saw things to eat inside –

custard pudding and cold chicken and tongue – and pies – and jam. It's rather a high window – but with wings –'

'How clever of you!' said Jane.

'Not at all,' said Cyril modestly; 'any born general – Napoleon or the Duke of Marlborough – would have seen it just the same as I did.'

'It seems very wrong,' said Anthea.

'Nonsense,' said Cyril. 'What was it Sir Philip Sidney said when the soldier wouldn't stand him a drink? – "My necessity is greater than his".'

'We'll club our money, though, and leave it to pay for the things, won't we?' Anthea was persuasive, and very nearly in tears, because it is most trying to feel enormously hungry and unspeakably sinful at one and the same time.

'Some of it,' was the cautious reply.

Everyone now turned out its pockets on the lead roof of the tower, where visitors for the last hundred and fifty years had cut their own and their sweethearts' initials with penknives in the soft lead. There was five-and-sevenpence-halfpenny altogether, and even the upright Anthea admitted that that was too much to pay for four people's dinners. Robert said he thought eightpence.

And a half-a-crown was finally agreed to be 'handsome'.

So Anthea wrote on the back of her last term's report, which happened to be in her pocket, and from which she first tore her own name and that of the school, the following letter:

DEAR REVEREND CLERGYMAN,

We are very hungry indeed because of having to fly all day, and we think it is not stealing when you are starving to death. We are afraid to ask you for fear you should say 'No,' because of course you know about angels, but you would not think we were angels. We will only take the necessities of life, and no pudding or pie, to show you it is not greediness but true starvation that makes us make your larder stand and deliver. But we are not highwaymen by trade.

'Cut it short,' said the others with one accord. And Anthea hastily added:

Our intentions are quite honourable if you only knew. And here is half-a-crown to show we are sinseer and grateful. Thank you for your kind hospitality.

FROM US FOUR.

The half-crown was wrapped in this letter, and all the children felt that when the clergyman had read it he would understand everything, as well as anyone could who had not seen the wings.

'Now,' said Cyril, 'of course there's some risk; we'd better fly straight down the other side of the tower and then flutter low across the churchyard and in through the shrubbery. There doesn't seem to be anyone about. But you never know. The window looks out into the shrubbery. It is embowered in foliage, like a window in a story. I'll go in and get the things. Robert and Anthea can take them as I hand them out through the window; and Jane can keep watch – her eyes are sharp – and whistle if she sees anyone about. Shut up, Robert! she can whistle quite well enough for that, anyway. It ought not to be a very good whistle – it'll sound more natural and birdlike. Now then – off we go!'

I cannot pretend that stealing is right. I can only say that on this occasion it did not look like stealing to the hungry four, but appeared in the light of a fair and reasonable business transaction. They had never happened to learn that a tongue – hardly cut into – a chicken and a half, a loaf of bread, and a syphon of soda-water cannot be bought in shops for half-a-crown. These were the necessaries of life which Cyril handed out of the larder window when, quite unobserved and without hindrance or adventure, he had led the others to that happy spot. He felt that to refrain from jam, apple turnovers, cake, and mixed candied peel was a really heroic act – and I agree with him. He was also proud of not taking the custard pudding – and there I think he was wrong – because if he had taken it there would have been a difficulty about returning the dish; no one, however starving, has a right to steal china pie-dishes with little pink flowers on them. The soda-water syphon was different. They could not do without something to drink, and as the maker's name was on it they felt sure it could be returned to him wherever they might leave it. If they had time they would take it back themselves. The man appeared to live in Rochester, which would not be much out of their way home.

Everything was carried up to the top of the tower, and laid down on a sheet of kitchen paper which Cyril had found on the top shelf of the larder. As he unfolded it, Anthea said, 'I don't think *that's* a necessity of life.'

'Yes, it is,' said he. 'We must put the things down somewhere to cut them up; and I heard father say the other day people get diseases from germans in rain-water. Now there must be lots of rain-water here – and when it dries up the germans are left, and they'd get into the things, and we should all die of scarlet fever.'

'What are germans?'

'Little waggly things you see with microscopes,' said Cyril, with a scientific air. 'They give you every illness you can think of. I'm sure the paper was a necessary, just as much as the bread and meat and water. Now then! Oh, my eyes, I am hungry!'

I do not wish to describe the picnic party on top of the tower. You can imagine well enough what it is like to carve a chicken and a tongue with a knife that has only one blade – and that snapped off short about half-way down. But it was done. Eating with your fingers is greasy and difficult – and paper dishes soon get to look very spotty and horrid. But one thing you *can't* imagine, and that is how soda-water behaves when you try to drink it straight out of a syphon – especially a quite full one. But if imagination will not help you, experience will, and you can easily try it for yourself if you can get a grown-up to give you the syphon. If you want to have a really thorough experience, put the tube in your mouth and press the handle very suddenly and very hard. You had better do it when you are alone – and out of doors is best for this experiment.

However you eat them, tongue and chicken and new bread are very good things, and no one minds being sprinkled a little with

These were the necessaries of life which Cyril
handed out of the larder window

'So help me,' he cried, 'if they ain't a pack of kiddies!'

The leader was the most glorious creature Robert had ever seen

. . . Jakin looked on with an expression of open-mouthed horror . . .

soda-water on a really fine hot day. So that everyone enjoyed the dinner very much indeed, and everyone ate as much as it possibly could: first, because it was extremely hungry; and secondly, because as I said, tongue and chicken and new bread are very nice.

Now, I daresay you will have noticed that if you have to wait for your dinner till long after the proper time, and then eat a great deal more dinner than usual, and sit in the hot sun on the top of a church-tower – or even anywhere else – you become soon and strangely sleepy. Now Anthea and Jane and Cyril and Robert were very like you in many ways, and when they had eaten all they could, and drunk all there was, they became sleepy, strangely and soon – especially Anthea, because she had got up so early.

One by one they left off talking and leaned back, and before it was a quarter of an hour after dinner they had all curled round and tucked themselves up under their large soft warm wings and were fast asleep. And the sun was sinking slowly in the west. (I must say it was in the west, because it is usual in books to say so, for fear careless people should think it was setting in the east. In point of fact, it was not exactly in the west either – but that's near enough.) The sun, I repeat, was sinking slowly in the west, and the children slept warmly and happily on – for wings are cosier than eiderdown quilts to sleep under. The shadow of the church-tower fell across the churchyard, and across the Vicarage, and across the field beyond; and presently there were no more shadows, and the sun had set, and the wings were gone. And still the children slept. But not for long. Twilight is very beautiful, but it is chilly; and you know, however sleepy you are, you wake up soon enough if your brother or sister happens to be up first and pulls your blankets off you. The four wingless children shivered and awoke. And there they were – on top of a church-tower in the dusky twilight, with blue stars coming out by ones and twos and tens and twenties over their heads – miles away from home, with three-and-three-halfpence in their pockets, and a doubtful act about the necessities of life to be accounted for if anyone found them with the soda-water syphon.

They looked at each other. Cyril spoke first, picking up the syphon:

'We'd better get along down and get rid of this beastly thing. It's dark enough to leave it on the clergyman's doorstep, I should think. Come on.'

There was a little turret at the corner of the tower, and the little turret had a door in it. They had noticed this when they were eating, but had not explored it, as you would have done in their place. Because, of course, when you have wings, and can explore the whole sky, doors seem hardly worth exploring.

Now they turned towards it.

'Of course,' said Cyril, 'this is the way down.'

It was. But the door was locked on the inside!

And the world was growing darker and darker. And they were miles from home. And there was the soda-water syphon.

I shall not tell you whether anyone cried, nor if so, how many cried, nor who cried. You will be better employed in making up your minds what you would have done if you had been in their place.

Chapter V

No Wings

Whether anyone cried or not, there was certainly an interval during which none of the party was quite itself. When they grew calmer, Anthea put her handkerchief in her pocket and her arm round Jane, and said:

'It can't be for more than one night. We can signal with our handkerchiefs in the morning. They'll be dry then. And someone will come up and let us out –'

'And find the syphon,' said Cyril gloomily; 'and we shall be sent to prison for stealing –'

'You said it wasn't stealing. You said you were sure it wasn't.'

'I'm not sure *now*,' said Cyril shortly.

'Let's throw the beastly thing slap away among the trees,' said Robert, 'then no one can do anything to us.'

'Oh yes' – Cyril's laugh was not a lighthearted one – 'and hit some chap on the head, and be murderers as well as – as the other thing.'

'But we can't stay up here all night,' said Jane; 'and I want my tea.'

'You *can't* want your tea,' said Robert; 'you've only just had your dinner.'

'But I do want it,' she said; 'especially when you begin talking about stopping up here all night. Oh, Panther – I want to go home! I want to go home!'

'Hush, hush,' Anthea said. 'Don't, dear. It'll be all right, somehow. Don't, don't –'

'Let her cry,' said Robert desperately; 'if she howls loud enough, someone may hear and come and let us out.'

'And see the soda-water thing,' said Anthea swiftly. 'Robert, don't be a brute. Oh, Jane, do try to be a man! It's just the same for all of us.'

Jane did try to 'be a man' – and reduced her howls to sniffs.

There was a pause. Then Cyril said slowly, 'Look here. We must risk that syphon. I'll button it up inside my jacket – perhaps no one will notice it. You others keep well in front of me. There are lights in the clergyman's house. They've not gone to bed yet. We must just yell as loud as ever we can. Now all scream when I say three. Robert, you do the yell like the railway engine, and I'll do the coo-ee like father's. The girls can do as they please. One, two, three!'

A fourfold yell rent the silent peace of the evening, and a maid at one of the Vicarage windows paused with her hand on the blind-cord.

'One, two, three!' Another yell, piercing and complex, startled

the owls and starlings to a flutter of feathers in the belfry
below. The maid fled from the Vicarage window and ran down the
Vicarage stairs and into the Vicarage kitchen, and fainted as soon
as she had explained to the man-servant and the cook and the
cook's cousin that she had seen a ghost. It was quite untrue, of
course, but I suppose the girl's nerves were a little upset by
the yelling.

'One, two, three!' The Vicar was on his doorstep by this time,
and there was no mistaking the yell that greeted him.

'Goodness me,' he said to his wife, 'my dear, someone's being
murdered in the church! Give me my hat and a thick stick, and tell
Andrew to come after me. I expect it's the lunatic who stole the
tongue.'

The children had seen the flash of light when the Vicar opened
his front door. They had seen his dark form on the doorstep, and
they had paused for breath, and also to see what he would do.

When he turned back for his hat, Cyril said hastily:

'He thinks he only fancied he heard something. You don't half
yell. Now! One, two, three!'

It was certainly a whole yell this time, and the Vicar's wife flung
her arms round her husband and screamed a feeble echo of it.

'You shan't go!' she said, 'not alone. Jessie!' – the maid
unfainted and came out of the kitchen – 'send Andrew at once.
There's a dangerous lunatic in the church, and he must go immediately and catch it.'

'I expect he *will* catch it too,' said Jessie to herself as she went
through the kitchen door. 'Here, Andrew,' she said, 'there's some-

one screaming like mad in the church, and the missus says you're to go along and catch it.'

'Not alone, I won't,' said Andrew in low firm tones. To his master he merely said, 'Yes, sir.'

'You heard those screams?'

'I did think I noticed a sort of something,' said Andrew.

'Well, come on, then,' said the Vicar. 'My dear, I *must* go!' He pushed her gently into the sitting-room, banged the door, and rushed out, dragging Andrew by the arm.

A volley of yells greeted them. As it died into silence Andrew shouted, 'Hullo, you there! Did you call?'

'Yes,' shouted four far-away voices.

'They seem to be in the air,' said the Vicar. 'Very remarkable.'

'Where are you?' shouted Andrew: and Cyril replied in his deepest voice, very slowly and loud:

'CHURCH! TOWER! TOP!'

'Come down, then!' said Andrew; and the same voice replied:
'Can't! Door locked!'

'My goodness!' said the Vicar. 'Andrew, fetch the stable lantern. Perhaps it would be as well to fetch another man from the village.'

'With the rest of the gang about, very likely. No sir; if this 'ere ain't a trap – well, may I never! There's cook's cousin at the back door now. He's a keeper, sir, and used to dealing with vicious characters. And he's got his gun, sir.'

'Hullo there!' shouted Cyril from the church-tower; 'come up and let us out.'

'We're a-coming,' said Andrew. 'I'm a-going to get a police-man and a gun.'

'Andrew, Andrew,' said the Vicar, 'that's not quite the truth.'

'It's near enough, sir, for the likes of them.'

So Andrew fetched the lantern and the cook's cousin; and the Vicar's wife begged them all to be very careful.

They went across the churchyard – it was quite dark now – and as they went they talked. The Vicar was certain a lunatic was on the church-tower – the one who had written the mad letter, and taken the cold tongue and things. Andrew thought it was a 'trap'; the cook's cousin alone was calm. 'Great cry, little wool,' said he; 'dangerous chaps is quieter.' He was not at all afraid. But then he had a gun. That was why he was asked to lead the way up the worn steep dark steps of the church-tower. He did lead the way, with the lantern in one hand and the gun in the other. Andrew went next. He pretended afterwards that this was because he was braver than his master, but really it was because he thought of traps, and he did not like the idea of being behind the other for fear someone should come softly up behind him and catch hold of his legs in the dark. They went on and on, and round and round the little cork-screw staircase – then through the bell-ringers' loft, where the bell-ropes hung with soft furry ends like giant caterpillars – then up another stair into the belfry, where the big quiet bells are – and then on, up a ladder with broad steps – and then up a little stone stair. And at the top of that there was a little door. And the door was bolted on the stair side.

The cook's cousin, who was a gamekeeper, kicked at the door, and said:

'Hullo, you there!'

The children were holding on to each other on the other side of the door, and trembling with anxiousness – and very hoarse with their howls. They could hardly speak, but Cyril managed to reply huskily:

'Hullo, you there!'

'How did you get up there?'

It was no use saying 'We flew up,' so Cyril said:

'We got up – and then found the door was locked and we couldn't get down. Let us out – do.'

'How many of you are there?' asked the keeper.

'Only four,' said Cyril.

'Are you armed?'

'Are you what?'

'I've got my gun handy – so you'd best not try any tricks,' said the keeper. 'If we open the door, will you promise to come quietly down, and no nonsense?'

'Yes – oh YES!' said all the children together.

'Bless me,' said the Vicar, 'surely that was a female voice?'

'Shall I open the door, sir?' said the keeper. Andrew went down a few steps, 'to leave room for the others,' he said afterwards.

'Yes,' said the Vicar, 'open the door. Remember,' he said through the keyhole, 'we have come to release you. You will keep your promise to refrain from violence?'

'How this bolt do stick,' said the keeper; 'anyone 'ud think it hadn't been drawed for half a year.' As a matter of fact it hadn't.

When all the bolts were drawn, the keeper spoke deep-chested words through the keyhole.

'I don't open,' said he, 'till you've gone over to the other side of the tower. And if one of you comes at me I fire. Now!'

'We're all over on the other side,' said the voices.

The keeper felt pleased with himself, and owned himself a bold man when he threw open that door, and, stepping out into the leads, flashed the full light of the stable lantern on to the group of desperadoes standing against the parapet on the other side of the tower.

He lowered his gun, and he nearly dropped the lantern.

'So help me,' he cried, 'if they ain't a pack of kiddies!'

The Vicar now advanced.

'How did you come here?' he asked severely. 'Tell me at once.'

'Oh, take us down,' said Jane, catching at his coat, 'and we'll tell you anything you like. You won't believe us, but it doesn't matter, Oh, take us down!'

The others crowded round him, with the same entreaty. All but Cyril. He had enough to do with the soda-water syphon, which would keep slipping down under his jacket. It needed both hands to keep it steady in its place.

But he said, standing as far out of the lantern light as possible: 'Please do take us down.'

So they were taken down. It is no joke to go down a strange church-tower in the dark, but the keeper helped them – only Cyril had to be independent because of the soda-water syphon. It would keep trying to get away. Half-way down the ladder it all but escaped. Cyril just caught it by its spout, and as nearly as possible lost his footing. He was trembling and pale when at last they reached the bottom of the winding stair and stepped out on to the flags of the church-porch.

Then suddenly the keeper caught Cyril and Robert each by an arm.

'You bring along the gells, sir,' said he; 'you and Andrew can manage them.'

'Let go!' said Cyril; 'we aren't running away. We haven't hurt your old church. Leave go!'

'You just come along,' said the keeper; and Cyril dared not oppose him with violence, because just then the syphon began to slip again.

So they were all marched into the Vicarage study, and the Vicar's wife came rushing in.

'Oh, William, *are* you safe?' she cried.

Robert hastened to allay her anxiety.

'Yes,' he said, 'he's quite safe. We haven't hurt him at all. And please, we're very late, and they'll be anxious at home. Could you send us home in your carriage?'

'Or perhaps there's a hotel near where we could get a carriage from,' said Anthea. 'Martha will be very anxious as it is.'

The Vicar had sunk into a chair, overcome by emotion and amazement.

Cyril had also sat down, and was leaning forward with his elbows on his knees because of that soda-water syphon.

'But how did you come to be locked up in the church-tower?' asked the Vicar.

'We went up,' said Robert slowly, 'and we were tired, and we all went to sleep, and when we woke up we found the door was locked, so we yelled.'

'I should think you did!' said the Vicar's wife. 'Frightening everybody out of their wits like this! You ought to be ashamed of yourselves.'

'We *are*,' said Jane gently.

'But who locked the door?' asked the Vicar.

'I don't know at all,' said Robert, with perfect truth. 'Do please send us home.'

'Well, really,' said the Vicar, 'I suppose we'd better. Andrew, put the horse to, and you can take them home.'

'Not alone, I don't,' said Andrew to himself.

'And,' the Vicar went on, 'let this be a lesson to you . . .' He went on talking, and the children listened miserably. But the keeper was not listening. He was looking at the unfortunate Cyril. He knew all about poachers, of course, so he knew how people look when they're hiding something. The Vicar had just got to the part about trying to grow up to be a blessing to your parents, and not a trouble and a disgrace, when the keeper suddenly said:

'Arst him what he's got there under his jacket'; and Cyril knew that concealment was at an end. So he stood up, and squared his shoulders and tried to look noble, like the boys in books that no one can look in the face of and doubt that they come of brave and noble families, and will be faithful to the death, and he pulled out the soda-water syphon and said:

'Well, there you are, then.'

There was a silence. Cyril went on – there was nothing else for it:

'Yes, we took this out of your larder, and some chicken and tongue and bread. We were very hungry, and we didn't take the custard or jam. We only took bread and meat and water – and we couldn't help its being the soda kind – just the necessaries of life; and we left half-a-crown to pay for it, and we left a letter. And we're very sorry. And my father will pay a fine or anything you like, but don't send us to prison. Mother would be so vexed. You know what you said about not being a disgrace. Well, don't you go and do it to us – that's all. We're as sorry as we can be. There!'

'However did you get up to the larder window?' said Mrs Vicar.

'I can't tell you that,' said Cyril firmly.

'Is this the whole truth you've been telling me?' asked the clergyman.

'No,' answered Jane suddenly; 'it's all true, but it's not the whole truth. We can't tell you that. It's no good asking. Oh, do forgive us and take us home!' She ran to the Vicar's wife and threw her arms round her. The Vicar's wife put her arms round Jane, and the keeper whispered behind his hand to the Vicar:

'They're all right, sir – I expect it's a pal they're standing by. Someone put 'em up to it, and they won't peach. Game little kids.'

'Tell me,' said the Vicar kindly, 'are you screening someone else? Had anyone else anything to do with this?'

'Yes,' said Anthea, thinking of the Psammead, 'but it wasn't their fault.'

'Very well, my dears,' said the Vicar, 'then let's say no more about it. Only just tell us why you wrote such an odd letter.'

'I don't know,' said Cyril. 'You see, Anthea wrote it in such a hurry, and it really didn't seem like stealing then. But afterwards, when we found we couldn't get down off the church-tower, it seemed just exactly like it. We are all very sorry –'

'Say no more about it,' said the Vicar's wife; 'but another time just think before you take other people's tongues. Now – some cake and milk before you go home?'

When Andrew came to say that the horse was put to, and was he expected to be led alone into the trap that he had plainly seen from the first, he found the children eating cake and drinking milk and laughing at the Vicar's jokes. Jane was sitting on the vicar's wife's lap.

So you see they got off better than they deserved.

The gamekeeper, who was the cook's cousin, asked leave to drive home with them, and Andrew was only too glad to have someone to protect him from the trap he was so certain of.

When the waggonette reached their own house, between the chalk-quarry and the gravel-pit, the children were very sleepy, but they felt that they and the keeper were friends for life.

Andrew dumped the children down at the iron gate without a word.

'You get along home,' said the Vicarage cook's cousin, who was a gamekeeper. 'I'll get me home on Shanks' mare.'

So Andrew had to drive off alone, which he did not like at all, and it was the keeper that was cousin to the Vicarage cook who went with the children to the door, and, when they had been swept to bed in a whirlwind of reproaches, remained to explain to Martha and the cook and the housemaid exactly what had happened. He explained so well that Martha was quite amicable the next morning.

After that he often used to come over to see Martha, and in the end – but that is another story, as dear Mr Kipling says.

Martha was obliged to stick to what she had said the night before about keeping the children indoors the next day for a punishment. But she wasn't at all snarky about it, and agreed to let Robert go out for half an hour to get something he particularly wanted.

This, of course, was the day's wish.

Robert rushed to the gravel-pit, found the Psammead, and presently wished for –

But that, too, is another story.

Chapter VI

A Castle and No Dinner

The others were to be kept in as a punishment for the misfortunes of the day before. Of course Martha thought it was naughtiness, and not misfortune – so you must not blame her. She only thought she was doing her duty. You know grown-up people often say they do not like to punish you, and they only do it for your own good, and that it hurts them as much as it hurts you – and this is really very often the truth.

Martha certainly hated having to punish the children quite as much as they hated to be punished. For one thing, she knew what a noise there would be in the house all day. And she had other reasons.

'I declare,' she said to the cook, 'it seems almost a shame keeping of them indoors this lovely day; but they are that audacious, they'll be walking in with their heads knocked off some of these days, if I don't put my foot down. You make them a cake for tea tomorrow, dear. And we'll have Baby along of us as we've got a bit forrard with our work. Then they can have a good romp with him out of the way. Now, Eliza, come, get on with them beds. Here's ten o'clock nearly, and no rabbits caught!'

People say that in Kent when they mean 'and no work done'.

So all the others were kept in, but Robert, as I have said, was allowed to go out for half an hour to get something they all wanted. And that, of course, was the day's wish.

He had no difficulty in finding the Sand-fairy, for the day was already so hot that it had actually, for the first time, come out of its own accord; it was sitting in a sort of pool of soft sand, stretching itself, and trimming its whiskers, and turning its snail's eyes round and round.

'Ha!' it said when its left eye saw Robert; 'I've been looking out for you. Where are the rest of you? Not smashed themselves up with those wings, I hope?'

'No,' said Robert; 'but the wings got us into a row, just like all the wishes always do. So the others are kept indoors, and I was only let out for half an hour – to get the wish. So please let me wish as quickly as I can.'

'Wish away,' said the Psammead, twisting itself round in the sand. But Robert couldn't wish away. He forgot all the things he had been thinking about, and nothing would come into his head but little things for himself, like toffee, a foreign stamp album, or a clasp-knife with three blades and a corkscrew. He sat down to think better, but it was no use. He could only think of things the others would not have cared for – such as a football, or a pair of leg-guards, or to be able to lick Simpkins minor thoroughly when he went back to school.

'Well,' said the Psammead at last, 'you'd better hurry up with that wish of yours. Time flies.'

'I know it does,' said Robert. '*I* can't think what to wish for. I wish you could give one of the others their wish without their having to come here to ask for it. Oh, *don't!*'

But it was too late. The Psammead had blown itself out to about three times its proper size, and now it collapsed like a pricked bubble, and with a deep sigh leaned back against the edge of its sand-pool, quite faint with the effort.

'There!' it said in a weak voice; 'it was tremendously hard – but I did it. Run along home, or they're sure to wish for something silly before you get there.'

They were – quite sure; Robert felt this, and as he ran home his mind was deeply occupied with the sort of wishes he might find they had wished in his absence. They might wish for rabbits, or white mice, or chocolate, or a fine day tomorrow, or even – and that was most likely – someone might have said, 'I do wish to goodness Robert would hurry up.' Well, he *was* hurrying up, and so they would have their wish, and the day would be wasted. Then he tried to think what they could wish for – something that would be amusing indoors. That had been his own difficulty from the beginning. So few things are amusing indoors when the sun is shining outside and you mayn't go out, however much you want to.

Robert was running as fast as he could, but when he turned the

corner that ought to have brought him within sight of the architect's nightmare – the ornamental iron-work on the top of the
house – he opened his eyes so wide that he had to drop into a walk;
for you cannot run with your eyes wide open. Then suddenly he
stopped short, for there was no house to be seen. The front-garden
railings were gone too, and where the house had stood – Robert
rubbed his eyes and looked again. Yes, the others *had* wished –
there was little doubt about that – and they must have wished that
they lived in a castle; for there the castle stood, black and stately,
and very tall and broad, with battlements and lancet windows, and
eight great towers; and, where the garden and orchard had been,
there were white things dotted like mushrooms. Robert walked
slowly on, and as he got nearer he saw that these were tents, and
men in armour were walking about among the tents – crowds and
crowds of them.

'Oh, crikey!' said Robert fervently. 'They *have!* They've wished
for a castle, and it's being besieged! It's just like that Sand-fairy! I
wish we'd never seen the beastly thing!'

At the little window above the great archway, across the moat
that now lay where the garden had been but half an hour ago,
someone was waving something pale dust-coloured. Robert
thought it was one of Cyril's handkerchiefs. They had never been
white since the day when he had upset the bottle of 'Combined
Toning and Fixing Solution' into the drawer where they were.
Robert waved back, and immediately felt that he had been unwise.
For his signal had been seen by the besieging force, and two men
in steel-caps were coming towards him. They had high brown

boots on their long legs, and they came towards him with such great strides that Robert remembered the shortness of his own legs and did not run away. He knew it would be useless to himself, and he feared it might be irritating to the foe. So he stood still – and the two men seemed quite pleased with him.

'By my halidom,' said one, 'a brave varlet this!'

Robert felt pleased at being *called* brave, and somehow it made him *feel* brave. He passed over the 'varlet'. It was the way people talked in historical romances for the young, he knew, and it was evidently not meant for rudeness. He only hoped he would be able to understand what they said to him. He had not always been able quite to follow the conversations in the historical romances for the young.

'His garb is strange,' said the other. 'Some outlandish treachery, belike.'

'Say, lad, what brings thee hither?'

Robert knew this meant, 'Now then, youngster, what are you up to here, eh?' – so he said:

'If you please, I want to go home.'

'Go, then!' said the man in the longest boots; 'none hindereth, and nought lets us to follow. Zooks!' he added in a cautious undertone, 'I misdoubt me but he beareth tidings to the besieged.'

'Where dwellest thou, young knave?' inquired the man with the largest steel-cap.

'Over there,' said Robert; and directly he had said it he knew he ought to have said 'Yonder!'

'Ha – sayest so?' rejoined the longest boots. 'Come hither, boy. This is a matter for our leader.'

And to the leader Robert was dragged forthwith – by the reluctant ear.

The leader was the most glorious creature Robert had ever seen. He was exactly like the pictures Robert had so often admired in the historical romances. He had armour, and a helmet, and a horse, and a crest, and feathers, and a shield, and a lance, and a sword. His armour and his weapons were all, I am almost sure, of quite different periods. The shield was thirteenth-century, while the sword was of the pattern used in the Peninsular War. The cuirass was of the time of Charles I, and the helmet dated from the Second Crusade. The arms on the shield were very grand – three red running lions on a blue ground. The tents were of the latest brand and the whole appearance of camp, army, and leader might have been a shock to some. But Robert was dumb with admiration, and it all seemed to him perfectly correct, because he knew no more of heraldry or archæology than the gifted artists who usually drew the pictures for the historical romances. The scene was indeed 'exactly like a picture'. He admired it all so much that he felt braver than ever.

'Come hither, lad,' said the glorious leader, when the men in Cromwellian steel-caps had said a few low eager words. And he took off his helmet, because he could not see properly with it on. He had a kind face, and long fair hair. 'Have no fear; thou shalt take no scathe,' he said.

Robert was glad of that. He wondered what 'scathe' was, and if it was nastier than the senna-tea which he had to take sometimes.

'Unfold thy tale without alarm,' said the leader kindly. 'Whence comest thou, and what is thine intent?'

'My what?' said Robert.

'What seekest thou to accomplish? What is thine errand, that thou wanderest here alone among these rough men-at-arms? Poor child, thy mother's heart aches for thee e'en now, I'll warrant me.'

'I don't think so,' said Robert; 'you see, she doesn't know I'm out.'

The leader wiped away a manly tear, exactly as a leader in a historical romance would have done, and said:

'Fear not to speak the truth, my child; thou hast nought to fear from Wulfric de Talbot.'

Robert had a wild feeling that this glorious leader of the besieging party – being himself part of a wish – would be able to understand better than Martha, or the gipsies, or the policeman in Rochester, or the clergyman of yesterday, the true tale of the ⸜wishes and the Psammead. The only difficulty was that he knew he could never remember enough 'quothas' and 'beshrew me's', and things like that, to make his talk sound like the talk of a boy in a historical romance. However, he began boldly enough, with a sentence straight out of *Ralph de Courcy*; or, *The Boy Crusader*. He said:

'Grammercy for the courtesy, fair sir knight. The fact is, it's like this – and I hope you're not in a hurry, because the story's rather a breather. Father and mother are away, and when we were down playing in the sand-pits we found a Psammead.'

'I cry thee mercy! A Sammyadd?' said the knight.

'Yes, a sort of – of fairy, or enchanter – yes, that's it, an enchanter; and he said we could have a wish every day, and we wished first to be beautiful.'

'Thy wish was scarce granted,' muttered one of the men-at-arms, looking at Robert, who went on as if he had not heard, though he thought the remark very rude indeed.

'And then we wished for money – treasure, you know; but we couldn't spend it. And yesterday we wished for wings, and we got them, and we had a ripping time to begin with –'

'Thy speech is strange and uncouth,' said Sir Wulfric de Talbot. 'Repeat thy words – what hadst thou?'

'A ripping – I mean a jolly – no – we were contented with our lot – that's what I mean; only after we got into an awful fix.'

'What is a fix? A fray, mayhap?'

'No – not a fray. A – a – a tight place.'

'A dungeon? Alas for thy youthful fettered limbs!' said the knight, with polite sympathy.

'It wasn't a dungeon. We just – just encountered undeserved misfortunes,' Robert explained, 'and today we are punished by not being allowed to go out. That's where I live' – he pointed to the castle. 'The others are in there, and they're not allowed to go out. It's all the Psammead's – I mean the enchanter's fault. I wish we'd never seen him.'

'He is an enchanter of might?'

'Oh yes – of might and main. Rather!'

'And thou deemest that it is the spells of the enchanter whom thou hast angered that have lent strength to the besieging party,' said the gallant leader; 'but know thou that Wulfric de Talbot needs no enchanter's aid to lead his followers to victory.'

'No, I'm sure you don't,' said Robert with hasty courtesy; 'of course not – you wouldn't, you know. But, all the same, it's partly his fault, but we're most to blame. You couldn't have done anything if it hadn't been for us.'

'How now, bold boy?' asked Sir Wulfric haughtily. 'Thy speech is dark, and eke scarce courteous. Unravel me this riddle!'

'Oh,' said Robert desperately, 'of course you don't know it, but you're not *real* at all. You're only here because the others must have been idiots enough to wish for a castle – and when the sun sets you'll just vanish away, and it'll be all right.'

The captain and the men-at-arms exchanged glances, at first pitying, and then sterner, as the longest-booted man said, 'Beware, noble my lord; the urchin doth but feign madness to escape from our clutches. Shall we not bind him?'

'I'm no more mad than you are,' said Robert angrily; 'perhaps not so much – only, I was an idiot to think you'd understand anything. Let me go – I haven't done anything to you.'

'Whither?' asked the knight, who seemed to have believed all the enchanter story till it came to his own share in it. 'Whither wouldst thou wend?'

'Home, of course,' Robert pointed to the castle.

'To carry news of succour? Nay!'

'All right, then,' said Robert, struck by a sudden idea; 'then let me go somewhere else.' His mind sought eagerly among his memories of the historical romance.

'Sir Wulfric de Talbot,' he said slowly, 'should think foul scorn to – to keep a chap – I mean, one who has done him no hurt – when he wants to cut off quietly – I mean, to depart without violence.'

'This to my face! Beshrew thee for a knave!' replied Sir Wulfric. But the appeal seemed to have gone home. 'Yet thou sayest sooth,' he added thoughtfully. 'Go where thou wilt,' he added nobly, 'thou art free. Wulfric de Talbot warreth not with babes, and Jakin here shall bear thee company.'

'All right,' said Robert wildly. 'Jakin will enjoy himself, I think. Come on, Jakin. Sir Wulfric, I salute thee.'

He saluted after the modern military manner, and set off running to the sand-pit, Jakin's long boots keeping up easily.

He found the Fairy. He dug it up, he woke it up, he implored it to give him one more wish.

'I've done two today already,' it grumbled, 'and one was as stiff a bit of work as ever I did.'

'Oh, do, do, do, do, *do!*' said Robert, while Jakin looked on with an expression of open-mouthed horror at the strange beast that talked, and gazed with its snail's eyes at him.

'Well, what is it?' snapped the Psammead, with cross sleepiness.

'I wish I was with the others,' said Robert. And the Psammead began to swell. Robert never thought of wishing the castle and siege away. Of course he knew they had all come out of a wish, but swords and daggers and pikes and lances seemed much too real to be wished away. Robert lost consciousness for an instant. When he opened his eyes the others were crowding round him.

'We never heard you come in,' they said. 'How awfully jolly of you to wish it to give us our wish!'

'Of course we understood that was what you'd done.'

'But you ought to have told us. Suppose we'd wished something silly.'

'Silly?' said Robert very crossly indeed. 'How much sillier could you have been, I'd like to know? You nearly settled *me* – I can tell you.'

Then he told his story, and the others admitted that it certainly had been rough on him. But they praised his courage and cleverness so much that he presently got back his lost temper, and felt braver than ever, and consented to be captain of the besieged force.

'We haven't done anything yet,' said Anthea comfortingly; 'we waited for you. We're going to shoot at them through these little loopholes with the bow and arrows uncle gave you, and you shall have first shot.'

'I don't think I would,' said Robert cautiously; 'you don't know what they're like near to. They've got *real* bows and arrows – an awful length – and swords and pikes and daggers, and all sorts of sharp things. They're all quite, quite real. It's not just a – a picture, or a vision, or anything; they can hurt us - or kill us even, I shouldn't wonder. I can feel my ear all sore still. Look here – have you explored the castle? Because I think we'd better let them alone as long as they let us alone. I heard that Jakin man say they weren't going to attack till just before sundown. We can be getting ready for the attack. Are there any soldiers in the castle to defend it?'

'We don't know,' said Cyril. 'You see, directly I'd wished we were in a besieged castle, everything seemed to go upside down, and when it came straight we looked out of the window, and saw the camp and things and you – and of course we kept on looking at everything. Isn't this room jolly? It's as real as real!'

It was. It was square, with stone walls four feet thick, and great beams for ceiling. A low door at the corner led to a flight of steps, up and down. The children went down; they found themselves in a great arched gatehouse – the enormous doors were shut and barred. There was a window in a little room at the bottom of the round turret up which the stair wound, rather larger than the other windows, and looking through it they saw that the drawbridge was up and the portcullis down; the moat looked very wide and deep. Opposite the great door that led to the moat was another great door, with a little door in it. The children went through this, and found themselves in a big paved courtyard, with the great grey walls of the castle rising dark and heavy on all four sides.

Near the middle of the courtyard stood Martha, moving her right hand backwards and forwards in the air. The cook was stooping down and moving her hands, also in a very curious way. But the oddest and at the same time most terrible thing was the Lamb, who was sitting on nothing, about three feet from the ground, laughing happily.

The children ran towards him. Just as Anthea was reaching out her arms to take him, Martha said crossly, 'Let him alone – do, miss, when he is good.'

'But what's he *doing*?' said Anthea.

'Doing? Why, a-sitting in his high chair as good as gold, a precious, watching me doing of the ironing. Get along with you, do – my iron's cold again.'

She went towards the cook and seemed to poke an invisible fire with an unseen poker – the cook seemed to be putting an unseen dish into an invisible oven.

'Run along with you, do,' she said; 'I'm behindhand as it is. You won't get no dinner if you come a-hindering of me like this. Come, off you goes, or I'll pin a dishcloth to some of your tails.'

'You're *sure* the Lamb's all right?' asked Jane anxiously.

'Right as ninepence, if you don't come unsettling of him. I thought you'd like to be rid of him for today; but take him, if you want, for gracious' sake.'

'No, no,' they said, and hastened away. They would have to defend the castle presently, and the Lamb was safer even suspended in mid-air in an invisible kitchen than in the guardroom of a besieged castle. They went through the first doorway they came to and sat down helplessly on a wooden bench that ran along the room inside.

'How awful!' said Anthea and Jane together; and Jane added, 'I feel as if I was in a mad asylum.'

'What does it mean?' Anthea said. 'It's creepy; I don't like it. I wish we'd wished for something plain – a rocking-horse, or a donkey, or something.'

'It's no use wishing *now*,' said Robert bitterly; and Cyril said: 'Do dry up a sec; I want to think.'

He buried his face in his hands, and the others looked about them. They were in a long room with an arched roof. There were wooden tables along it, and one across at the end of the room, on a sort of raised platform. The room was very dim and dark. The floor was strewn with dry things like sticks, and they did not smell nice.

Cyril sat up suddenly and said:

'Look here – it's all right. I think it's like this. You know, we wished that the servants shouldn't notice any difference when we got wishes. And nothing happens to the Lamb unless we specially wish it to. So of course they don't notice the castle or anything. But then the castle is on the same place where our house was – is, I mean – and the servants have to go on being in the house, or else they would notice. But you can't have a castle mixed up with our house – and so we can't see the house, because we see the castle; and they can't see the castle, because they go on seeing the house; and so –'

'Oh, *don't!*' said Jane; 'you make my head go all swimmy, like being on a roundabout. It doesn't matter! Only, I hope we shall be able to see our dinner, that's all – because if it's invisible it'll be unfeelable as well, and then we can't eat it! I *know* it will, because I tried to feel if I could feel the Lamb's chair, and there was nothing under him at all but air. And we can't eat air, and I feel just as if I hadn't any breakfast for years and years.'

'It's no use thinking about it,' said Anthea. 'Let's go on exploring. Perhaps we might find something to eat.'

This lighted hope in every breast, and they went on exploring the castle. But though it was the most perfect and delightful castle you can possibly imagine, and furnished in the most complete and beautiful manner, neither food nor men-at-arms were to be found in it.

'If only you'd thought of wishing to be besieged in a castle thoroughly garrisoned and provisioned!' said Jane reproachfully.

'You can't think of everything, you know,' said Anthea. 'I should think it must be nearly dinner-time by now.'

It wasn't; but they hung about watching the strange movements of the servants in the middle of the courtyard, because, of course, they couldn't be sure where the dining-room of the invisible house was. Presently they saw Martha carrying an invisible tray across the courtyard, for it seemed that, by the most fortunate accident, the dining-room of the house and the banqueting-hall of the castle were the same place. But oh, how their hearts sank when they perceived that the tray was invisible!

They waited in wretched silence while Martha went through the form of carving an unseen leg of mutton and serving invisible greens and potatoes with a spoon that no one could see. When she had left the room, the children looked at the empty table, and then at each other.

'This is worse than anything,' said Robert, who had not till now been particularly keen on his dinner.

'I'm not so very hungry,' said Anthea, trying to make the best of things, as usual.

Cyril tightened his belt ostentatiously. Jane burst into tears.

Chapter VII

A SIEGE AND BED

The children were sitting in the gloomy banqueting-hall, at the end of one of the long bare wooden tables. There was now no hope. Martha had brought in the dinner, and the dinner was invisible, and unfeelable too; for, when they rubbed their hands along the table, they knew but too well that for them there was nothing there *but* table.

Suddenly Cyril felt in his pocket.

'Right, *oh!*' he cried. 'Look here! Biscuits.'

Rather broken and crumbled, certainly, but still biscuits. Three whole ones, and a generous handful of crumbs and fragments.

'I got them this morning – cook – I'd quite forgotten,' he explained as he divided them with scrupulous fairness into four heaps.

They were eaten in happy silence, though they tasted a little oddly, because they had been in Cyril's pocket all the morning with a hunk of tarred twine, some green fir-cones, and a ball of cobbler's wax.

'Yes, but look here, Squirrel,' said Robert; 'you're so clever at explaining about invisibleness and all that. How is it the biscuits are here, and all the bread and meat and things have disappeared?'

'I don't know,' said Cyril after a pause, 'unless it's because *we* had them. Nothing about us has changed. Everything's in my pocket all right.'

'Then if we *had* the mutton it would be real,' said Robert. 'Oh, don't I wish we could find it!'

'But we can't find it. I suppose it isn't ours till we've got it in our mouths.'

'Or in our pockets,' said Jane, thinking of the biscuits.

'Who puts mutton in their pockets, goose-girl?' said Cyril. 'But I know – at any rate, I'll try it!'

He leaned over the table with his face about an inch from it, and kept opening and shutting his mouth as if he were taking bites out of air.

'It's no good,' said Robert in deep dejection. 'You'll only – Hullo!'

Cyril stood up with a grin of triumph, holding a square piece of bread in his mouth. It was quite real. Everyone saw it. It is true that, directly he bit a piece off, the rest vanished; but it was all right, because he knew he had it in his hand though he could neither see nor feel it. He took another bite from the air between his fingers, and it turned into bread as he bit. The next moment all the others were following his example, and opening and shutting their mouths an inch or so from the bare-looking table. Robert captured a slice of mutton, and – but I think I will draw a veil over the rest of this painful scene. It is enough to say that they all had enough mutton, and that when Martha came to change the plates she said she had never seen such a mess in all her born days.

The pudding was, fortunately, a plain suet roly-poly, and in answer to Martha's questions, the children all with one accord said that they would *not* have treacle on it – nor jam, nor sugar –'Just plain, please,' they said. Martha said, 'Well, I never – what next, I wonder!' and went away.

Then ensued another scene on which I will not dwell, for nobody looks nice picking up slices of suet pudding from the table in its mouth, like a dog.

The great thing, after all, was that they had had dinner; and now everyone felt more courage to prepare for the attack that was to be delivered before sunset. Robert, as captain, insisted on climbing to the top of one of the towers to reconnoitre, so up they all went. And now they could see all round the castle, and could see, too, that beyond the moat, on every side, the tents of the besieging party were pitched. Rather uncomfortable shivers ran down the children's backs as they saw that all the men were busy cleaning or sharpening their arms, re-stringing their bows, and polishing their shields. A large party came along the road, with horses dragging along the great trunk of a tree; and Cyril felt quite pale, because he knew this was for a battering-ram.

'What a good thing we've got a moat,' he said; 'and what a good thing the drawbridge is up – I should never have known how to work it.'

'Of course it would be up in a besieged castle.'

*A trumpeter came forward . . . and blew the longest
and loudest blast they had yet heard*

He lifted up the baker's boy and set him on the top of the haystack

*. . . it was at the head of an enthusiastic procession that
Robert entered the trampled meadow where the Fair was held . . .*

. . . a little dark moustache appeared . . .

'You'd think there ought to have been soldiers in it, wouldn't you?' said Robert.

'You see you don't know how long it's been besieged,' said Cyril darkly; 'perhaps most of the brave defenders were killed quite early in the siege and all the provisions eaten, and now there are only a few intrepid survivors – that's us, and we are going to defend it to the death.'

'How do you begin – defending to the death, I mean?' asked Anthea.

'We ought to be heavily armed – and then shoot at them when they advance to the attack.'

'They used to pour boiling lead down on besiegers when they got too close,' said Anthea. 'Father showed me the holes on purpose for pouring it down through at Bodiam Castle. And there are holes like it in the gate-tower here.'

'I think I'm glad it's only a game; it *is* only a game, isn't it?' said Jane.

But no one answered.

The children found plenty of strange weapons in the castle, and if they were armed at all it was soon plain that they would be, as Cyril said, 'armed heavily' – for these swords and lances and crossbows were far too weighty even for Cyril's manly strength; and as for the longbows, none of the children could even begin to bend them. The daggers were better; but Jane hoped that the besiegers would not come close enough for daggers to be of any use.

'Never mind, we can hurl them like javelins,' said Cyril, 'or drop them on people's heads. I say – there are lots of stones on the other side of the courtyard. If we took some of those up? Just to drop on their heads if they were to try swimming the moat.'

So a heap of stones grew apace, up in the room above the gate; and another heap, a shiny spiky dangerous-looking heap, of daggers and knives.

As Anthea was crossing the courtyard for more stones, a sudden and valuable idea came to her.

She went to Martha and said, 'May we have just biscuits for tea? we're playing at besieged castles, and we'd like the biscuits to provision the garrison. Put mine in my pocket, please, my hands are so dirty. And I'll tell the others to fetch theirs.'

This was indeed a happy thought, for now with four generous handfuls of air, which turned to biscuits as Martha crammed it into their pockets, the garrison was well provisioned till sundown.

They brought up some iron pots of cold water to pour on the besiegers instead of hot lead, with which the castle did not seem to be provided.

The afternoon passed with wonderful quickness. It was very exciting; but none of them, except Robert, could feel all the time that this was real deadly dangerous work. To the others, who had only seen the camp and the besiegers from a distance, the whole thing seemed half a game of make-believe, and half a splendidly distinct and perfectly safe dream. But it was only now and then that Robert could feel this.

When it seemed to be tea-time the biscuits were eaten with water from the deep well in the courtyard, drunk out of horns.

Cyril insisted on putting by eight of the biscuits, in case anyone should feel faint in stress of battle.

Just as he was putting away the reserve biscuits in a sort of little stone cupboard without a door, a sudden sound made him drop three. It was the loud fierce cry of a trumpet.

'You see, it *is* real,' said Robert, 'and they are going to attack.'

All rushed to the narrow windows.

'Yes,' said Robert, 'they're all coming out of their tents and moving about like ants. There's that Jakin dancing about where the bridge joins on. I wish he could see me put my tongue out at him. Yah!'

The others were far too pale to wish to put their tongues out at anybody. They looked at Robert with surprised respect. Anthea said:

'You really *are* brave, Robert.'

'Rot!' Cyril's pallor turned to redness now, all in a minute. 'He's been getting ready to be brave all the afternoon. And I wasn't ready, that's all. I shall be braver than he is in half a jiffy.'

'Oh dear!' said Jane, 'what does it matter which of you is the bravest? I think Cyril was a perfect silly to wish for a castle, and I don't want to play.'

'It *isn't*' – Robert was beginning sternly, but Anthea interrupted –

'Oh yes, you do,' she said coaxingly; 'it's a very nice game, really, because they can't possibly get in, and if they do the women and children are always spared by civilised armies.'

'But are you quite, quite sure they *are* civilised?' asked Jane, panting. 'They seem to be such a long time ago.'

'Of course they are.' Anthea pointed cheerfully through the narrow window. 'Why look at the little flags on their lances, how bright they are – and how fine the leader is! Look, that's him – isn't it, Robert? – on the grey horse.'

Jane consented to look, and the scene was almost too pretty to be alarming. The green turf, the white tents, the flash of pennoned lances, the gleam of armour, and the bright colours of scarf and tunic – it was just like a splendid coloured picture. The trumpets were sounding, and when the trumpets stopped for breath the children could hear the cling-clang of armour and the murmur of voices.

A trumpeter came forward to the edge of the moat, which now seemed very much narrower than at first, and blew the longest and loudest blast they had yet heard. When the blaring noise had died away, a man who was with the trumpeter shouted:

'What ho, within there!' and his voice came plainly to the garrison in the gate-house.

'Hullo there!' Robert bellowed back at once.

'In the name of our Lord the King, and of our good lord and trusty leader Sir Wulfric de Talbot, we summon this castle to surrender – on pain of fire and sword and no quarter. Do ye surrender?'

'No,' bawled Robert, 'of course we don't! Never, *Never, NEVER!*'

The man answered back:

'Then your fate be on your own heads.'

'Cheer,' said Robert in a fierce whisper. 'Cheer to show them we aren't afraid, and rattle the daggers to make more noise. One, two, three! Hip, hip, hooray! Again – Hip, hip, hooray! One more – Hip, hip, hooray!' The cheers were rather high and weak, but the rattle of the daggers lent them strength and depth.

There was another shout from the camp across the moat – and then the beleaguered fortress felt that the attack had indeed begun.

It was getting rather dark in the room above the great gate, and Jane took a very little courage as she remembered that sunset *couldn't* be far off now.

'The moat is dreadfully thin,' said Anthea.

'But they can't get into the castle even if they do swim over,' said Robert. And as he spoke he heard feet on the stair outside – heavy feet and the clank of steel. No one breathed for a moment. The steel and the feet went on up the turret stairs. Then Robert sprang softly to the door. He pulled off his shoes.

'Wait here,' he whispered, and stole quickly and softly after the boots and the spur-clank. He peeped into the upper room. The man was there – and it was Jakin, all dripping with moat-water, and he was fiddling about with the machinery which Robert felt sure worked the drawbridge. Robert banged the door suddenly, and turned the great key in the lock, just as Jakin sprang to the inside of the door. Then he tore downstairs and into the little turret at the foot of the tower where the biggest window was.

'We ought to have defended *this*!' he cried to the others as they followed him. He was just in time. Another man had swum over, and his fingers were on the window-ledge. Robert never knew how the man had managed to climb up out of the water. But he saw the clinging fingers, and hit them as hard as he could with an iron bar that he caught up from the floor. The man fell with a plop-splash into the moat-water. In another moment Robert was outside the little room, had banged its door and was shooting home the enormous bolts, and calling to Cyril to lend a hand.

Then they stood in the arched gate-house, breathing hard and looking at each other.

Jane's mouth was open.

'Cheer up, Jenny,' said Robert, – 'it won't last much longer.'

There was a creaking above, and something rattled and shook. The pavement they stood on seemed to tremble. Then a crash told them that the drawbridge had been lowered to its place.

'That's that beast Jakin,' said Robert. 'There's still the port-cullis; I'm almost certain that's worked from lower down.'

And now the drawbridge rang and echoed hollowly to the hoofs of horses and the tramp of armed men.

'Up – quick!' cried Robert. 'Let's drop things on them.'

Even the girls were feeling almost brave now. They followed Robert quickly, and under his directions began to drop stones out through the long narrow windows. There was a confused noise below, and some groans.

'Oh dear!' said Anthea, putting down the stone she was just going to drop out. 'I'm afraid we've hurt somebody!'

Robert caught up the stone in a fury.

'I should just hope we *had!*' he said. 'I'd give something for a jolly good boiling kettle of lead. Surrender, indeed!'

And now came more tramping, and a pause, and then the thundering thump of the battering-ram. And the little room was almost quite dark.

'We've held it,' cried Robert, 'we *won't* surrender! The sun *must* set in a minute. Here – they're all jawing underneath again. Pity there's no time to get more stones! Here, pour that water down on them. It's no good, of course, but they'll hate it.'

'Oh dear!' said Jane; 'don't you think we'd better surrender?'

'Never!' said Robert; 'we'll have a parley if you like, but we'll never surrender. Oh, I'll be a soldier when I grow up – you just see if I don't. I won't go into the Civil Service, whatever anyone says.'

'Let's wave a handkerchief and ask for a parley,' Jane pleaded. 'I don't believe the sun's going to set tonight at all.'

'Give them the water first – the brutes!' said the bloodthirsty Robert. So Anthea tilted the pot over the nearest lead-hole, and poured. They heard a splash below, but no one below seemed to have felt it. And again the ram battered the great door. Anthea paused.

'How idiotic,' said Robert, lying flat on the floor and putting one eye to the lead-hole, 'Of course the holes go straight down into the gate-house – that's for when the enemy has got past the door and the portcullis, and almost all is lost. Here, hand me the pot.' He crawled on to the three-cornered window-ledge in the middle of the wall, and, taking the pot from Anthea, poured the water out through the arrow-slit.

And as he began to pour, the noise of the battering-ram and the trampling of the foe and the shouts of 'Surrender!' and 'De Talbot for ever!' all suddenly stopped and went out like the snuff of a candle; the little dark room seemed to whirl round and turn topsy-turvy, and when the children came to themselves there they were, safe and sound, in the big front bedroom of their own house – the house with the ornamental nightmare iron-top to the roof.

They all crowded to the window and looked out. The moat and the tents and the besieging force were all gone – and there was the garden with its tangle of dahlias and marigolds and asters and late roses, and the spiky iron railings and the quiet white road.

Everyone drew a deep breath.

'And that's all right!' said Robert. 'I told you so! And, I say, we didn't surrender, did we?'

'Aren't you glad now I wished for a castle?' asked Cyril.

'I think I am *now*,' said Anthea slowly. 'But I wouldn't wish for it again, I think, Squirrel dear!'

'Oh, it was simply splendid!' said Jane unexpectedly. 'I wasn't frightened a bit.'

'Oh, I say!' Cyril was beginning, but Anthea stopped him.

'Look here,' she said, 'it's just come into my head. This is the very first thing we've wished for that hasn't got us into a row. And there hasn't been the least little scrap of a row about this. Nobody's raging downstairs, we're safe and sound, we've had an awfully jolly day – at least not jolly exactly, but you know what I mean. And we know now how brave Robert is – and Cyril too, of course,' she added hastily, 'and Jane as well. And we haven't got into a row with a single grown-up.'

The door was opened suddenly and fiercely.

'You ought to be ashamed of yourselves,' said the voice of Martha, and they could tell by her voice that she was very angry indeed. 'I thought you couldn't last through the day without getting up to some doggery! A person can't take a breath of air on the front doorstep but you must be emptying the wash-hand jug on to their heads! Off you go to bed, the lot of you, and try to get up better children in the morning. Now then – don't let me have to tell you twice. If I find any of you not in bed in ten minutes I'll let you know it, that's all! A new cap, and everything!'

She flounced out amid a disregarded chorus of regrets and apologies. The children were very sorry, but really it was not their faults. You can't help it if you are pouring water on a besieging foe, and your castle suddenly changes into your house – and everything changes with it except the water, and that happens to fall on somebody else's clean cap.

'I don't know why the water didn't change into nothing, though,' said Cyril.

'Why should it?' asked Robert. 'Water's water all the world over.'

'I expect the castle well was the same as ours in the stable-yard,' said Jane. And that was really the case.

'I thought we couldn't get through a wish-day without a row,' said Cyril; 'it was too good to be true. Come on, Bobs, my military hero. If we lick into bed sharp she won't be so frumious, and haps she'll bring us up some supper. I'm jolly hungry! Good-night, kids.'

'Good-night. I hope the castle won't come creeping back in the night,' said Jane.

'Of course it won't,' said Anthea briskly, 'but Martha will – not in the night, but in a minute. Here, turn round, I'll get that knot out of your pinafore strings.'

'Wouldn't it have been degrading for Sir Wulfric de Talbot,' said Jane dreamily, 'if he could have known that half the besieged garrison wore pinafores?'

'And the other half knickerbockers. Yes – frightfully. Do stand still – you're only tightening the knot,' said Anthea.

Chapter VIII

Bigger Than the Baker's Boy

'Look here,' said Cyril. 'I've got an idea.'

'Does it hurt much?' said Robert sympathetically.

'Don't be a jackape! I'm not humbugging.'

'Shut up, Bobs!' said Anthea.

'Silence for the Squirrel's oration,' said Robert.

Cyril balanced himself on the edge of the water-butt in the back yard, where they all happened to be, and spoke.

'Friends, Romans, countrymen – and women – we found a Sammyadd. We have had wishes. We've had wings, and being beautiful as the day – ugh! – that was pretty jolly beastly if you like – and wealth and castles, and that rotten gipsy business with the Lamb. But we're no forrader. We haven't really got anything worth having for our wishes.'

'We've had things happening,' said Robert, 'that's always something.'

'It's not enough, unless they're the right things,' said Cyril firmly. 'Now I've been thinking –'

'Not really?' whispered Robert.

'In the silent what's-its-names of the night. It's like suddenly being asked something out of history – the date of the Conquest or something; you know it all right all the time, but when you're asked it all goes out of your head. Ladies and gentlemen, you know jolly well that when we're all rotting about in the usual way heaps of things keep cropping up, and then real earnest wishes come into the heads of the beholder –'

'Here, here!' said Robert.

'– of the beholder, however stupid he is,' Cyril went on. 'Why, even Robert might happen to think of a really useful wish if he didn't injure his poor little brains trying so hard to think. – Shut up, Bobs, I tell you – You'll have the whole show over.'

A struggle on the edge of a water-butt is exciting, but damp. When it was over, and the boys were partially dried, Anthea said:

'It really was you began it, Bobs. Now honour is satisfied, do let Squirrel go on. We're wasting the whole morning.'

'Well then,' said Cyril, still wringing the water out of the tails of his jacket, 'I'll call it pax if Bobs will.'

'Pax then,' said Robert sulkily. 'But I've got a lump as big as a cricket ball over my eye.'

Anthea patiently offered a dust-coloured handkerchief, and Robert bathed his wounds in silence. 'Now Squirrel,' she said.

'Well then – let's just play bandits, or forts, or soldiers, or any of the old games. We're dead sure to think of something if we try not to. You always do.'

The others consented. Bandits were hastily chosen for the

game. 'It's as good as anything else,' said Jane gloomily. It must be owned that Robert was at first but a half-hearted bandit, but when Anthea had borrowed from Martha the red spotted handkerchief in which the keeper had brought her mushrooms that morning, and had tied up Robert's head with it so that he could be the wounded hero who had saved the bandit captain's life the day before, he cheered up wonderfully. All were soon armed. Bows and arrows slung on the back look well; and umbrellas and cricket stumps stuck through the belt give a fine impression of the wearer's being armed to the teeth. The white cotton hats that men wear in the country nowadays have a very brigandish effect when a few turkey's feathers are stuck in them. The Lamb's mail-cart was covered with a red-and-blue checked tablecloth, and made an admirable baggage-waggon. The Lamb asleep inside of it was not at all in the way. So the banditti set out along the road that led to the sand-pit.

'We ought to be near the Sammyadd,' said Cyril, 'in case we think of anything suddenly.'

It is all very well to make up your minds to play bandits – or chess, or ping-pong, or any other agreeable game – but it is not easy to do it with spirit when all the wonderful wishes you can think of, or can't think of, are waiting for you round the corner. The game was dragging a little, and some of the bandits were beginning to feel that the others were disagreeable things, and were saying so candidly, when the baker's boy came along the road with loaves in a basket. The opportunity was not one to be lost.

'Stand and deliver!' cried Cyril.

'Your money or your life!' said Robert.

And they stood on each side of the baker's boy. Unfortunately he did not seem to enter into the spirit of the thing at all. He was a baker's boy of an unusually large size. He merely said:

'Chuck it now, d'ye hear!' and pushed the bandits aside most disrespectfully.

Then Robert lassoed him with Jane's skipping-rope, and instead of going round his shoulders, as Robert intended, it went round his feet and tripped him up. The basket was upset, the beautiful new loaves went bumping and bouncing all over the dusty chalky road. The girls ran to pick them up, and all in a moment Robert and the baker's boy were fighting it out, man to man, with Cyril to see fair play, and the skipping-rope twisting round their legs like an interested snake that wished to be a peacemaker. It did not succeed; indeed the way the boxwood handles sprang up and hit the fighters on the shins and ankles was not at all peace-making. I know this is the second fight – or contest – in this chapter, but I can't help it. It was that sort of day. You know yourself there are days when rows seem to keep on happening, quite without your meaning them to. If I were a writer of tales of adventure such as those which used to appear in *The Boys of England* when I was young, of course I should be able to describe the fight, but I cannot do it. I never can see what happens during a fight, even when it is only dogs. Also, if I had been one of these *Boys of England* writers, Robert would have got the best of it. But I am like George Washington – I cannot tell a lie, even about a cherry-tree, much less about a fight, and I cannot conceal from you that Robert was badly beaten, for the second time that day. The baker's boy blacked his other eye, and, being ignorant of the first rules of fair play and gentlemanly behaviour, he also pulled Robert's hair, and kicked him on the knee. Robert always used to say he could have licked the butcher if it hadn't been for the girls. But I am not sure. Anyway, what happened was this, and very painful it was to self-respecting boys.

Cyril was just tearing off his coat so as to help his brother in proper style, when Jane threw her arms round his legs and began to cry and ask him not to go and be beaten too. That 'too' was very nice for Robert, as you can imagine – but it was nothing to what he felt when Anthea rushed in between him and the baker's boy, and caught that unfair and degraded fighter round the waist, imploring him not to fight any more.

'Oh, don't hurt my brother any more!' she said in floods of tears. 'He didn't mean it – it's only play. And I'm sure he's very sorry.'

You see how unfair this was to Robert. Because, if the baker's boy had had any right and chivalrous instincts, and had yielded to Anthea's pleading and accepted her despicable apology, Robert could not, in honour, have done anything to him at a future time. But Robert's fears, if he had any, were soon dispelled. Chivalry was a stranger to the breast of the baker's boy. He pushed Anthea away very roughly, and he chased Robert with kicks and unpleasant conversation right down the road to the sand-pit, and there, with one last kick, he landed him in a heap of sand.

'I'll larn you, you young varmint!' he said, and went off to pick up his loaves and go about his business. Cyril, impeded by Jane, could do nothing without hurting her, for she clung round his legs with the strength of despair. The baker's boy went off red and damp about the face; abusive to the last, he called them a pack of silly idiots, and disappeared round the corner. Then Jane's grasp loosened. Cyril turned away in silent dignity to follow Robert, and the girls followed him, weeping without restraint.

It was not a happy party that flung itself down in the sand beside the sobbing Robert. For Robert was sobbing – mostly with rage. Though of course I know that a really heroic boy is always dry-eyed after a fight. But then he always wins, which had not been the case with Robert.

Cyril was angry with Jane; Robert was furious with Anthea; the girls were miserable; and not one of the four was pleased with the baker's boy. There was, as French writers say, 'a silence full of emotion'.

Then Robert dug his toes and his hands into the sand and wriggled in his rage. 'He'd better wait till I'm grown up – the cowardly brute! Beast! – I hate him! But I'll pay him out. Just because he's bigger than me.'

'You began,' said Jane incautiously.

'I know I did, silly – but I was only rotting – and he kicked me – look here –'

Robert tore down a stocking and showed a purple bruise touched up with red.

'I only wish I was bigger than him, that's all.'

He dug his fingers in the sand, and sprang up, for his hand had touched something furry. It was the Psammead, of course – 'On the look-out to make sillies of them as usual,' as Cyril remarked later. And of course the next moment Robert's wish was granted, and he was bigger than the baker's boy. Oh, but much, much bigger. He was bigger than the big policeman who used to be at the crossing at the Mansion House years ago – the one who was so kind in helping old ladies over the crossing – and he was the biggest man *I* have ever seen, as well as the kindest. No one had a foot-rule in its pocket, so Robert could not be measured – but he was taller than your father would be if he stood on your mother's head, which I am sure he would never be unkind enough to do. He must have been ten or eleven feet high, and as broad as a boy of that height ought to be. His Norfolk suit had fortunately grown too, and now he stood up in it – with one of his enormous stockings turned down to show the gigantic bruise on his vast leg. Immense tears of fury still stood on his flushed giant face. He looked so surprised, and he was so large to be wearing an Eton collar, that the others could not help laughing.

'The Sammyadd's done us again,' said Cyril.

'Not us – *me*,' said Robert. 'If you'd got any decent feeling you'd try to make it make you the same size. You've no idea how silly it feels,' he added thoughtlessly.

'And I don't want to; I can jolly well see how silly it looks,' Cyril was beginning; but Anthea said:

'Oh, *don't*! I don't know what's the matter with you boys today. Look here, Squirrel, let's play fair. It is hateful for poor old Bobs, all alone up there. Let's ask the Sammyadd for another wish, and, if it will, I do really think we ought to be made the same size.'

The others agreed, but not gaily; but when they found the Psammead, it wouldn't.

'Not I,' it said crossly, rubbing its face with it feet. 'He's a rude violent boy, and it'll do him good to be the wrong size for a bit. What did he want to come digging me out with his nasty wet hands for? He nearly touched me! He's a perfect savage. A boy of the Stone Age would have had more sense.'

Robert's hands had indeed been wet – with tears.

'Go away and leave me in peace, do,' the Psammead went on. 'I can't think why you don't wish for something sensible – something to eat or drink, or good manners, or good tempers. Go along with you, do!'

It almost snarled as it shook its whiskers, and turned a sulky brown back on them. The most hopeful felt that further parley was in vain.

They turned again to the colossal Robert.

'Whatever shall we do?' they said; and they all said it.

'First,' said Robert grimly, 'I'm going to reason with that baker's boy. I shall catch him at the end of the road.'

'Don't hit a chap littler than yourself, old man,' said Cyril.

'Do I look like hitting him?' said Robert scornfully. 'Why, I should *kill* him. But I'll give him something to remember. Wait till I pull up my stocking.' He pulled up his stocking, which was as large as a small bolster-case, and strode off. His strides were six or seven feet long, so that it was quite easy for him to be at the bottom of the hill, ready to meet the baker's boy when he came down swinging the empty basket to meet his master's cart, which had been leaving bread at the cottages along the road.

Robert crouched behind a haystack in the farmyard, that is at the corner, and when he heard the boy come whistling along he jumped out at him and caught him by the collar.

'Now,' he said, and his voice was about four times its usual size, just as his body was four times its, 'I'm going to teach you to kick boys smaller than you.'

He lifted up the baker's boy and set him on the top of the haystack, which was about sixteen feet from the ground, and then he sat down on the roof of the cowshed and told the baker's boy exactly what he thought of him. I don't think the boy heard it all – he was in a sort of trance of terror. When Robert had said everything he could think of, and some things twice over, he shook the boy and said:

'And now get down the best way you can,' and left him.

I don't know how the baker's boy got down, but I do know that he missed the cart, and got into the hottest of hot water when he turned up at last at the bakehouse. I am sorry for him, but, after all, it was quite right that he should be taught that English boys mustn't use their feet when they fight, but their fists. Of course the water he got into only became hotter when he tried to tell his master about the boy he had licked and the giant as high as a church, because no one could possibly believe such a tale as that. Next day the tale was believed – but that was too late to be of any use to the baker's boy.

When Robert rejoined the others he found them in the garden. Anthea had thoughtfully asked Martha to let them have dinner out there – because the dining-room was rather small, and it would have been so awkward to have a brother the size of Robert in there. The Lamb, who had slept peacefully during the whole stormy morning, was now found to be sneezing, and Martha said he had a cold and would be better indoors.

'And really it's just as well,' said Cyril, 'for I don't believe he'd ever have stopped screaming if he'd once seen you the awful size you are!'

Robert was indeed what a draper would call an 'out-size' in boys. He found himself able to step right over the iron gate in the front garden.

Martha brought out the dinner – it was cold veal and baked potatoes, with sago pudding and stewed plums to follow.

She of course did not notice that Robert was anything but the usual size, and she gave him as much meat and potatoes as usual and no more. You have no idea how small your usual helping of dinner looks when you are many times your proper size. Robert groaned, and asked for more bread. But Martha would not go on giving more bread for ever. She was in a hurry, because the keeper intended to call on his way to Benenhurst Fair, and she wished to be dressed smartly before he came.

'I wish *we* were going to the Fair,' said Robert.

'You can't go anywhere that size,' said Cyril.

'Why not?' said Robert. 'They have giants at fairs, much bigger ones than me.'

'Not much, they don't,' Cyril was beginning, when Jane screamed 'Oh!' with such loud suddenness that they all thumped her on the back and asked whether she had swallowed a plum-stone.

'No,' she said, breathless from being thumped, 'it's – it's not a plum-stone. It's an idea. Let's take Robert to the Fair, and get them to give us money for showing him! Then we really *shall* get something out of the old Sammyadd at last!'

'Take me indeed!' said Robert indignantly. 'Much more likely me take you!'

And so it turned out. The idea appealed irresistibly to everyone but Robert, and even he was brought round by Anthea's suggestion that he should have a double share of any money they might make. There was a little old pony-trap in the coach-house – the kind that is called a governess cart. It seemed desirable to get to the Fair as quickly as possible, so Robert – who could now take enormous steps and so go very fast indeed – consented to wheel the others in this. It was as easy to him now as wheeling the Lamb in the mail-cart had been in the morning. The Lamb's cold prevented his being of the party.

It was a strange sensation being wheeled in a pony-carriage by a giant. Everyone enjoyed the journey except Robert and the few people they passed on the way. These mostly went into what looked like some kind of standing-up fits by the roadside, as Anthea said. Just outside Benenhurst, Robert hid in a barn, and the others went on to the Fair.

There were some swings, and a hooting tooting blaring merry-go-round, and a shooting-gallery and coconut-shies. Resisting an impulse to win a coconut – or at least to attempt the enterprise –

Cyril went up to the woman who was loading little guns before the array of glass bottles on strings against a sheet of canvas.

'Here you are, little gentleman!' she said. 'Penny a shot!'

'No, thank you,' said Cyril, 'We are here on business, not on pleasure. Who's the master?'

'The what?'

'The master – the head – the boss of the show.'

'Over there,' she said, pointing to a stout man in a dirty linen jacket who was sleeping in the sun; 'but I don't advise you to wake him sudden. His temper's contrary, especially these hot days. Better to have a shot while you're waiting.'

'It's rather important,' said Cyril. 'It'll be very profitable to him. I think he'll be sorry if we take it away.'

'Oh, if it's money in his pocket,' said the woman. 'No kid now? What is it?'

'It's a *giant*.'

'You *are* kidding!'

'Come along and see,' said Anthea.

The woman looked doubtfully at them, then she called to a ragged little girl in striped stockings and a dingy white petticoat that came below her brown frock, and leaving her in charge of the 'shooting-gallery' she turned to Anthea and said, 'Well, hurry up! But if you *are* kidding, you'd best say so. I'm as mild as milk myself, but my Bill, he's a fair terror and –'

Anthea led the way to the barn. 'It really *is* a giant,' she said. 'He's a giant little boy – in Norfolks like my brother's there. And we didn't bring him up to the Fair because people do stare so, and they seem to go into kind of standing-up fits when they see him. And we thought perhaps you'd like to show him and get pennies; and if you like to pay us something, you can – only, it'll have to be rather a lot, because we promised him he should have a double share of whatever we made.'

The woman murmured something indistinct, of which the children could only hear the words, 'Swelp me!' 'balmy,' and 'crumpet,' which conveyed no definite idea to their minds.

She had taken Anthea's hand, and was holding it very firmly; and Anthea could not help wondering what would happen if Robert should have wandered off or turned his proper size during the interval. But she knew that the Psammead's gifts really did last till sunset, however inconvenient their lasting might be; and she did not think, somehow, that Robert would care to go out alone while he was that size.

When they reached the barn and Cyril called 'Robert!' there was a stir among the loose hay, and Robert began to come out. His hand and arm came first – then a foot and leg. When the woman saw the hand she said 'My!' but when she saw the foot she said 'Upon my civvy!' and when, by slow and heavy degrees, the whole of Robert's enormous bulk was at last completely disclosed, she drew a long breath and began to say many things, compared with which 'balmy' and 'crumpet' seemed quite ordinary. She dropped into understandable English at last.

'What'll you take for him?' she said excitedly. 'Anything in reason. We'd have a special van built – leastways, I know where there's a second-hand one would do up handsome – what a baby elephant had, as died. What'll you take? He's soft, ain't he? Them giants mostly is – but I never see – no never! What'll you take? Down on the nail. We'll treat him like a king, and give him first-rate grub and a doss fit for a bloomin' dook. He must be dotty or he wouldn't need you kids to cart him about. What'll you take for him?'

'They won't take anything,' said Robert sternly. 'I'm no more soft than you are – not so much, I shouldn't wonder. I'll come and be a show for today if you'll give me' – he hesitated at the enormous price he was about to ask – 'if you'll give me fifteen shillings.'

'Done,' said the woman, so quickly that Robert felt he had been unfair to himself, and wished he had asked thirty. 'Come on now – and see my Bill – and we'll fix a price for the season. I dessay you might get as much as two quid a week reg'lar. Come on – and make yourself as small as you can, for gracious' sake!'

This was not very small, and a crowd gathered quickly, so that it was at the head of an enthusiastic procession that Robert entered the trampled meadow where the Fair was held, and passed over the stubbly yellow dusty grass to the door of the biggest tent. He crept in, and the woman went to call her Bill. He was the big sleeping man, and he did not seem at all pleased at being awakened. Cyril, watching through a slit in the tent, saw him scowl and shake a heavy fist and a sleepy head. Then the woman went on speaking very fast. Cyril heard 'Strewth', and 'biggest draw you ever, so help me!' and he began to share Robert's feeling that fifteen shillings was indeed far too little. Bill slouched up to the tent and

entered. When he beheld the magnificent proportions of Robert
he said but little – 'Strike me pink!' were the only words the
children could afterwards remember – but he produced fifteen
shillings, mainly in sixpences and coppers, and handed it to
Robert.

'We'll fix up about what you're to draw when the show's over
tonight,' he said with coarse heartiness. 'Lor' love a duck! you'll
be that happy with us you'll never want to leave us. Can you do a
song now – or a bit of a breakdown?'

'Not today,' said Robert, rejecting the idea of trying to sing 'As
once in May', a favourite of his mother's, and the only song he
could think of at the moment.

'Get Levi and clear them bloomin' photos out. Clear the tent.
Stick up a curtain or suthink,' the man went on. 'Lor', what a pity
we ain't got no tights his size! But we'll have 'em before the week's
out. Young man, your fortune's made. It's a good thing you came
to me, and not to some chaps as I could tell you on. I've known
blokes as beat their giants, and starved 'em too; so I'll tell you
straight, you're in luck this day if you never was afore. 'Cos I'm a
lamb, I am – and I don't deceive you.'

'I'm not afraid of anyone's beating *me*,' said Robert, looking
down on the 'lamb'. Robert was crouched on his knees, because
the tent was not big enough for him to stand upright in, but even in
that position he could still look down on most people. 'But I'm
awfully hungry – I wish you'd get me something to eat.'

'Here, 'Becca,' said hoarse Bill. 'Get him some grub – the best
you've got, mind!' Another whisper followed, of which the

children only heard, 'Down in black and white – first thing tomorrow.'

Then the woman went to get the food – it was only bread and cheese when it came, but it was delightful to the large and empty Robert; and the man went to post sentinels round the tent, to give the alarm if Robert should attempt to escape with his fifteen shillings.

'As if we weren't honest,' said Anthea indignantly when the meaning of the sentinels dawned on her.

Then began a very strange and wonderful afternoon.

Bill was a man who knew his business. In a very little while, the photographic views, the spyglasses you look at them through so that they really seem rather real, and the lights you see them by, were all packed away. A curtain – it was an old red-and-black carpet really – was run across the tent. Robert was concealed behind, and Bill was standing on a trestle-table outside the tent making a speech. It was rather a good speech. It began by saying that the giant it was his privilege to introduce to the public that day was the eldest son of the Emperor of San Francisco, compelled through an unfortunate love affair with the Duchess of the Fiji Islands to leave his own country and take refuge in England – the land of liberty – where freedom was the right of every man, no matter how big he was. It ended by the announcement that the first twenty who came to the tent door should see the giant for three-pence apiece. 'After that,' said Bill, 'the price is riz, and I don't undertake to say what it won't be riz to. So now's yer time.'

A young man squiring his sweetheart on her afternoon out was the first to come forward. For that occasion his was the princely attitude – no expense spared – money no object. His girl wished to see the giant? Well, she should see the giant, even though seeing the giant cost threepence each and the other entertainments were all penny ones.

The flap of the tent was raised – the couple entered. Next moment a wild shriek from the girl thrilled all present. Bill slapped his leg. 'That's done the trick!' he whispered to 'Becca. It was indeed a splendid advertisement of the charms of Robert. When the girl came out she was pale and trembling, and a crowd was round the tent.

'What was it like?' asked a bailiff.

'Oh! – horrid! – you wouldn't believe,' she said. 'It's as big as a barn, and that fierce. It froze the blood in my bones. I wouldn't ha' missed seeing it for anything.'

The fierceness was only caused by Robert's trying not to laugh. But the desire to do that soon left him, and before sunset he was more inclined to cry than to laugh, and more inclined to sleep than either. For, by ones and twos and threes people kept coming in all the afternoon, and Robert had to shake hands with those who wished it, and to allow himself to be punched and pulled and patted and thumped, so that people might make sure he was really real.

The other children sat on a bench and watched and waited, and were very bored indeed. It seemed to them that this was the hardest way of earning money that could have been invented. And only fifteen shillings! Bill had taken four times that already, for the news of the giant had spread, and tradespeople in carts, and gentle-people in carriages, came from far and near. One gentleman with an eyeglass, and a very large yellow rose in his buttonhole, offered Robert, in an obliging whisper, ten pounds a week to appear at the Crystal Palace. Robert had to say 'No.'

'I can't,' he said regretfully. 'It's no use promising what you can't do.'

'Ah, poor fellow, bound up for a term of years, I suppose! Well, here's my card; when your time's up come to me.'

'I will – if I'm the same size then,' said Robert truthfully.

'If you grow a bit, so much the better,' said the gentleman.

When he had gone, Robert beckoned Cyril and said:

'Tell them I must and will have an easy. And I want my tea.'

Tea was provided, and a paper hastily pinned on the tent. It said:

CLOSED FOR HALF AN HOUR

WHILE THE GIANT GETS HIS TEA

Then there was a hurried council.

'How am I to get away?' said Robert. 'I've been thinking about it all the afternoon.'

'Why, walk out when the sun sets and you're your right size. They can't do anything to us.'

Robert opened his eyes. 'Why, they'd nearly kill us,' he said, 'when they saw me get my right size. No, we must think of some other way. We *must* be alone when the sun sets.'

'I know,' said Cyril briskly, and he went to the door, outside which Bill was smoking a clay pipe and talking in a low voice to 'Becca. Cyril heard him say – 'Good as havin' a fortune left you.'

'Look here,' said Cyril, 'you can let people come in again in a minute. He's nearly finished his tea. But he *must* be left alone when the sun sets. He's very queer at that time of day, and if he's worried I won't answer for the consequences.'

'Why – what comes over him?' asked Bill.

'I don't know; it's – it's a sort of a *change*,' said Cyril candidly. 'He ain't at all like himself – you'd hardly know him. He's very queer indeed. Someone'll get hurt if he's not alone about sunset.' This was true.

'He'll pull round for the evening, I s'pose?'

'Oh yes – half an hour after sunset he'll be quite himself again.'

'Best to humour him,' said the woman.

And so, at what Cyril judged was about half an hour before sunset, the tent was again closed, 'whilst the giant gets his supper.'

The crowd was very merry about the giant's meals and their coming so close together.

'Well, he can pick a bit,' Bill owned. 'You see, he has to eat hearty, being the size he is.'

Inside the tent the four children breathlessly arranged a plan of retreat.

'You go *now*,' said Cyril to the girls, and get along home as fast as you can. Oh, never mind the beastly pony-cart; we'll get that tomorrow. Robert and I are dressed the same. We'll manage somehow, like Sidney Carton did. Only, you girls *must* get out, or it's all no go. We can run, but you can't – whatever you may think.

No, Jane, it's no good Robert going out and knocking people down. The police would follow him till he turned his proper size, and then arrest him like a shot. Go you must! If you don't I'll never speak to you again. It was you got us into this mess really, hanging round people's legs the way you did this morning. *Go*, I tell you!'

And Jane and Anthea went.

'We're going home,' they said to Bill. 'We're leaving the giant with you. Be kind to him.' And that, as Anthea said afterwards, was very deceitful, but what were they to do?

When they had gone, Cyril went to Bill.

'Look here,' he said, 'he wants some ears of corn – there's some in the next field but one. I'll just run and get it. Oh, and he says can't you loop up the tent at the back a bit? He says he's stifling for a breath of air. I'll see no one peeps in at him. I'll cover him up, and he can take a nap while I go for the corn. He *will* have it – there's no holding him when he gets like this.'

The giant was made comfortable with a heap of sacks and an old tarpaulin. The curtain was looped up, and the brothers were left alone. They matured their plans in whispers. Outside, the merry-go-round blared out its comic tunes, screaming now and then to arrest public notice.

Half a minute after the sun had set, a boy in a Norfolk suit came out past Bill.

'I'm off for the corn,' he said, and mingled quickly with the crowd.

At the same instant a boy came out of the back of the tent past 'Becca, posted there as sentinel.

'I'm off after the corn,' said this boy also. And he, too, moved away quietly and was lost in the crowd. The front-door boy was Cyril; the back-door was Robert – now, since sunset, once more his proper size. They walked quickly through the field, and along the road, where Robert caught Cyril up. Then they ran. They were home as soon as the girls were, for it was a long way, and they ran most of it. It was indeed a *very* long way, as they found when they had to go and drag the pony-trap home next morning, with no enormous Robert to wheel them in it as if it were a mail-cart, and they were babies and he was their gigantic nursemaid.

·   ·   ·

I cannot possibly tell you what Bill and 'Becca said when they found that the giant had gone. For one thing, I do not know.

Chapter IX

GROWN UP

Cyril had once pointed out that ordinary life is full of occasions on which a wish would be most useful. And this thought filled his mind when he happened to wake early on the morning after the morning after Robert had wished to be bigger than the baker's boy, and had been it. The day that lay between these two days had been occupied entirely by getting the governess-cart home from Benenhurst.

Cyril dressed hastily; he did not take a bath, because tin baths are so noisy, and he had no wish to rouse Robert, and he slipped off alone, as Anthea had once done, and ran through the dewy morning to the sand-pit. He dug up the Psammead very carefully and kindly, and began the conversation by asking it whether it still felt any ill effects from the contact with the tears of Robert the day before yesterday. The Psammead was in a good temper. It replied politely.

'And now, what can I do for you?' it said. 'I suppose you've

But Martha was stronger than he. She lifted him
up and carried him into the house

'Ye seek a pow-wow?' he said in excellent English

come here so early to ask for something for yourself, something your brothers and sisters aren't to know about, eh? Now, do be persuaded for your own good! Ask for a good fat Megatherium and have done with it.'

'Thank you – not today, I think,' said Cyril cautiously. 'What I really wanted to say was – you know how you're always wishing for things when you're playing at anything?'

'I seldom play,' said the Psammead coldly.

'Well, you know what I mean,' Cyril went on impatiently. 'What I want to say is: won't you let us have our wish just when we think of it, and just where we happen to be? So that we don't have to come and disturb you again,' added the crafty Cyril.

'It'll only end in your wishing for something you don't really want, like you did about the castle,' said the Psammead, stretching its brown arms and yawning. 'It's always the same since people left off eating really wholesome things. However, have it your own way. Good-bye.'

'Good-bye,' said Cyril politely.

'I'll tell you what,' said the Psammead suddenly, shooting out its long snail's eyes – 'I'm getting tired of you – all of you. You have no more sense than so many oysters. Go along with you!'

And Cyril went.

'What an awful long time babies *stay* babies,' said Cyril after the Lamb had taken his watch out of his pocket while he wasn't noticing, and with coos and clucks of naughty rapture had opened the case and used the whole thing as a garden spade, and when even immersion in a wash-hand basin had failed to wash the mould from the works and made the watch go again. Cyril had said several things in the heat of the moment; but now he was calmer, and had even consented to carry the Lamb part of the way to the woods. Cyril had persuaded the others to agree to his plan, and not to wish for anything more till they really did wish it. Meantime it seemed good to go to the woods for nuts, and on the mossy grass under a sweet chestnut-tree the five were sitting. The Lamb was pulling up the moss by fat handfuls, and Cyril was gloomily contemplating the ruins of his watch.

'He does grow,' said Anthea. 'Doesn't oo, precious?'

'Me grow,' said the Lamb cheerfully – 'me grow big boy, have guns an' mouses – an' – an' . . .' Imagination or vocabulary gave out here. But anyway it was the longest speech the Lamb had ever made, and it charmed everyone, even Cyril, who tumbled the Lamb over and rolled him in the moss to the music of delighted squeals.

'I suppose he'll be grown up some day,' Anthea was saying, dreamily looking up at the blue of the sky that showed between the long straight chestnut-leaves. But at that moment the Lamb, struggling gaily with Cyril, thrust a stoutly-shod little foot against his brother's chest; there was a crack! – the innocent Lamb had broken the glass of father's second-best Waterbury watch, which Cyril had borrowed without leave.

'Grow up some day!' said Cyril bitterly, plumping the Lamb down on the grass. 'I daresay he will – when nobody wants him to. I wish to goodness he would –'

'*Oh*, take care!' cried Anthea in an agony of apprehension. But it was too late – like music to a song her words and Cyril's came out together –

Anthea – 'Oh, take care!'

Cyril – 'Grow up now!'

The faithful Psammead was true to its promise, and there before the horrified eyes of its brothers and sisters, the Lamb suddenly and violently grew up. It was the most terrible moment. The change was not so sudden as the wish-changes usually were. The Baby's face changed first. It grew thinner and larger, lines came in the forehead, the eyes grew more deep-set and darker in colour, the mouth grew longer and thinner; most terrible of all, a little dark moustache appeared on the lip of one who was still – except as to the face – a two-year-old baby in a linen smock and white open-work socks.

'Oh, I wish it wouldn't! Oh, I wish it wouldn't! You boys might wish as well!' They all wished hard, for the sight was enough to dismay the most heartless. They all wished so hard, indeed, that they felt giddy, and almost lost consciousness; but the wishing was quite vain, for, when the wood ceased to whirl round, their dazzled eyes were riveted at once by the spectacle of a very proper-looking young man in flannels and a straw hat – a young man who wore the same little black moustache which just before they had actually seen growing upon the Baby's lip. This, then, was the Lamb – grown up! Their own Lamb! It was a terrible moment. The grown-up Lamb moved gracefully across the moss and settled himself against the trunk of the sweet chestnut. He tilted the straw hat over his eyes. He was evidently weary. He was going to sleep. The Lamb – the original little tiresome beloved Lamb – often went to sleep at odd times and in unexpected places. Was this new Lamb in the grey flannel suit and the pale green necktie like the other Lamb? or had his mind grown up together with his body?

That was the question which the others, in a hurried council held among the yellowing bracken a few yards from the sleeper, debated eagerly.

'Whichever it is, it'll be just as awful,' said Anthea. 'If his inside senses are grown up too, he won't stand our looking after him; and if he's still a baby inside of him how on earth are we to get him to do anything? And it'll be getting on for dinner-time in a minute –'

'And we haven't got any nuts,' said Jane.

'Oh, bother nuts!' said Robert; 'but dinner's different – I didn't have half enough dinner yesterday. Couldn't we tie him to the tree and go home to our dinners and come back afterwards?'

'A fat lot of dinner we'd get if we went back without the Lamb!' said Cyril in scornful misery. 'And it'll be just the same if we go back with him in the state he is now. Yes, I know it's my doing; don't rub it in! I know I'm a beast, and not fit to live; you can take that for settled, and say no more about it. The question is, what are we going to do?'

'Let's wake him up, and take him into Rochester or Maidstone and get some grub at a pastrycook's,' said Robert hopefully.

'Take him?' repeated Cyril. 'Yes – do! It's all my fault – I don't deny that – but you'll find you've got your work cut out for you if you try to take that young man anywhere. The Lamb always was spoilt, but now he's grown up he's a demon – simply. I can see it. Look at his mouth.'

'Well, then,' said Robert, 'let's wake him up and see what *he'll* do. Perhaps *he'll* take us to Maidstone and stand Sam. He ought to have a lot of money in the pockets of those extra-special bags. We *must* have dinner, anyway.'

They drew lots with little bits of bracken. It fell to Jane's lot to waken the grown-up Lamb.

She did it gently by tickling his nose with a twig of wild honeysuckle. He said 'Bother the flies!' twice, and then opened his eyes.

'Hullo, kiddies!' he said in a languid tone, 'still here? What's the giddy hour? You'll be late for your grub!'

'I know we shall,' said Robert bitterly.

'Then cut along home,' said the grown-up Lamb.

'What about your grub, though?' asked Jane.

'Oh, how far is it to the station, do you think? I've a sort of notion that I'll run up to town and have some lunch at the club.'

Blank misery fell like a pall on the four others. The Lamb – alone – unattended – would go to town and have lunch at a club! Perhaps he would also have tea there. Perhaps sunset would come upon him amid the dazzling luxury of club-land, and a helpless cross sleepy baby would find itself alone amid unsympathetic waiters, and would wail miserably for 'Panty' from the depths of a club arm-chair! The picture moved Anthea almost to tears.

'Oh no, Lamb ducky, you mustn't do that!' she cried incautiously.

The grown-up Lamb frowned. 'My dear Anthea,' he said, 'how

often am I to tell you that my name is Hilary or St Maur or Devereux? – any of my baptismal names are free to my little brothers and sisters, but *not* "Lamb" – a relic of foolish and far-off childhood.'

This was awful. He was their elder brother now, was he? Well, of course he was, if he was grown up – since they weren't. Thus, in whispers, Anthea and Robert.

But the almost daily adventures resulting from the Psammead wishes were making the children wise beyond their years.

'Dear Hilary,' said Anthea, and the others choked at the name, 'you know father didn't wish you to go to London. He wouldn't like us to be left alone without you to take care of us. Oh, deceitful beast that I am!' she added to herself.

'Look here,' said Cyril, 'if you're our elder brother, why not behave as such and take us over to Maidstone and give us a jolly good blow-out, and we'll go on the river afterwards?'

'I'm infinitely obliged to you,' said the Lamb courteously, 'but I should prefer solitude. Go home to your lunch – I mean your dinner. Perhaps I may look in about tea-time – or I may not be home till after you are in your beds.'

Their beds! Speaking glances flashed between the wretched four. Much bed there would be for them if they went home without the Lamb.

'We promised mother not to lose sight of you if we took you out,' Jane said before the others could stop her.

'Look here, Jane,' said the grown-up Lamb, putting his hands in his pockets and looking down at her, 'little girls should be seen and not heard. You kids must learn not to make yourselves a nuisance. Run along home now – and perhaps, if you're good, I'll give you each a penny tomorrow.'

'Look here,' said Cyril, in the best 'man to man' tone at his command, 'where are you going, old man? You might let Bobs and me come with you – even if you don't want the girls.'

This was really rather noble of Cyril, for he never did care much about being seen in public with the Lamb, who of course after sunset would be a baby again.

The 'man to man' tone succeeded.

'I shall just run over to Maidstone on my bike,' said the new Lamb airily, fingering the little black moustache. 'I can lunch at The Crown – and perhaps I'll have a pull on the river; but I can't take you all on the machine – now, can I? Run along home, like good children.'

The position was desperate. Robert exchanged a despairing look with Cyril. Anthea detached a pin from her waistband, a pin whose withdrawal left a gaping chasm between skirt and bodice, and handed it furtively to Robert – with a grimace of the darkest and deepest meaning. Robert slipped away to the road. There, sure enough, stood a bicycle – a beautiful new free-wheel. Of course Robert understood at once that if the Lamb was grown up he *must* have a bicycle. This had always been one of Robert's own reasons for wishing to be grown up. He hastily began to use the pin – eleven punctures in the back tyre, seven in the front. He would have made the total twenty-two but for the rustling of the yellow hazel-leaves, which warned him of the approach of the others. He hastily leaned a hand on the wheel, and was rewarded by the 'whish' of what was left of the air escaping from eighteen neat pin-holes.

'Your bike's run down,' said Robert, wondering how he could so soon have learned to deceive.

'So it is,' said Cyril.

'It's a puncture,' said Anthea, stooping down, and standing up again with a thorn which she had got ready for the purpose. 'Look here.'

The grown-up Lamb (or Hilary, as I suppose one must now call him) fixed his pump and blew up the tyre. The punctured state of it was soon evident.

'I suppose there's a cottage somewhere near – where one could get a pail of water?' said the Lamb.

There was; and when the number of punctures had been made manifest, it was felt to be a special blessing that the cottage provided 'teas for cyclists'. It provided an odd sort of tea-and-hammy meal for the Lamb and his brothers. This was paid for out of the fifteen shillings which had been earned by Robert when he was a giant – for the Lamb, it appeared, had unfortunately no money about him. This was a great disappointment for the others; but it is a thing that will happen, even to the most grown-up of us. However, Robert had enough to eat, and that was something. Quietly but persistently the miserable four took it in turns to try to persuade the Lamb (or St Maur) to spend the rest of the day in the woods. There was not very much of the day left by the time he had mended the eighteenth puncture. He looked up from the completed work with a sigh of relief, and suddenly put his tie straight.

'There's a lady coming,' he said briskly – 'for goodness' sake, get out of the way. Go home – hide – vanish somehow! I can't be seen with a pack of dirty kids.' His brothers and sisters were indeed rather dirty, because, earlier in the day, the Lamb, in his infant state, had sprinkled a good deal of garden soil over them. The grown-up Lamb's voice was so tyrant-like, as Jane said afterwards, that they actually retreated to the back garden, and left him with his little moustache and his flannel suit to meet alone the young lady, who now came up the front garden wheeling a bicycle.

The woman of the house came out, and the young lady spoke to her – the Lamb raised his hat as she passed him – and the children could not hear what she said, though they were craning round the corner by the pig-pail and listening with all their ears. They felt it to be 'perfectly fair,' as Robert said, 'with that wretched Lamb in that condition.'

When the Lamb spoke, in a languid voice heavy with politeness, they heard well enough.

'A puncture?' he was saying. 'Can I not be of any assistance? If you could allow me – ?'

There was a stifled explosion of laughter behind the pig-pail – the grown-up Lamb (otherwise Devereux) turned the tail of an angry eye in its direction.

'You're very kind,' said the lady, looking at the Lamb. She looked rather shy, but, as the boys put it, there didn't seem to be any nonsense about her.

'But oh,' whispered Cyril behind the pig-pail, 'I should have thought he'd had enough bicycle-mending for one day – and if she only knew that really and truly he's only a whiny-piny, silly little baby!'

'He's *not*,' Anthea murmured angrily. 'He's a dear – if people only let him alone. It's our own precious Lamb still, whatever silly idiots may turn him into – isn't he, Pussy?'

Jane doubtfully supposed so.

Now, the Lamb – whom I must try to remember to call St Maur – was examining the lady's bicycle and talking to her with a very grown-up manner indeed. No one could possibly have supposed, to see and hear him, that only that very morning he had been a chubby child of two years breaking other people's Waterbury watches. Devereux (as he ought to be called for the future) took out a gold watch when he had mended the lady's bicycle, and all the onlookers behind the pig-pail said 'Oh!' because it seemed so unfair that the Baby who had only that morning destroyed two cheap but honest watches, should now, in the grown-upness Cyril's folly had raised him to, have a real gold watch – with a chain and seals!

Hilary (as I will now term him) withered his brothers and sisters with a glance, and then said to the lady – with whom he seemed to be quite friendly:

'If you will allow me, I will ride with you as far as the Cross Roads; it is getting late, and there are tramps about.'

No one will ever know what answer the young lady intended to give to this gallant offer, for, directly Anthea heard it made, she rushed out, knocking against the pig-pail, which overflowed in a turbid stream, and caught the Lamb (I suppose I ought to say

Hilary) by the arm. The others followed, and in an instant the four
dirty children were visible, beyond disguise.

'Don't let him,' said Anthea to the lady, and she spoke with
intense earnestness; 'he's not fit to go with anyone!'

'Go away, little girl!' said St Maur (as we will now call him) in a
terrible voice. 'Go home at once!'

'You'd much better not have anything to do with him,' the now
reckless Anthea went on. 'He doesn't know who he is. He's something very different from what you think he is.'

'What do you mean?' asked the lady not unnaturally, while
Devereux (as I must term the grown-up Lamb) tried vainly to push
Anthea away. The others backed her up, and she stood solid as a
rock.

'You just let him go with you,' said Anthea, 'you'll soon see
what I mean! How would you like to suddenly see a poor little
helpless baby spinning along downhill beside you with its feet up
on a bicycle it had lost control of?'

The lady had turned rather pale.

'Who are these very dirty children?' she asked the grown-up
Lamb (sometimes called St Maur in these pages).

'I don't know,' he lied miserably.

'Oh, Lamb! how *can* you?' cried Jane – 'when you know perfectly well you're our own little baby brother that we're so fond
of. We're his big brothers and sisters,' she explained, turning to
the lady, who with trembling hands was now turning her bicycle
towards the gate, 'and we've got to take care of him. And we must
get him home before sunset, or I don't know whatever will

become of us. You see, he's sort of under a spell – enchanted – you know what I mean!'

Again and again the Lamb (Devereux, I mean) had tried to stop Jane's eloquence, but Robert and Cyril held him, one by each leg, and no proper explanation was possible. The lady rode hastily away, and electrified her relatives at dinner by telling them of her escape from a family of dangerous lunatics. 'The little girl's eyes were simply those of a maniac. I can't think how she came to be at large,' she said.

When her bicycle had whizzed away down the road, Cyril spoke gravely.

'Hilary, old chap,' he said, 'you must have had a sunstroke or something. And the things you've been saying to that lady! Why, if we were to tell you the things you've said when you are yourself again, say tomorrow morning, you wouldn't even understand them – let alone believe them! You trust to me, old chap, and come home, now, and if you're not yourself in the morning we'll ask the milkman to ask the doctor to come.'

The poor grown-up Lamb (St Maur was really one of his Christian names) seemed now too bewildered to resist.

'Since you seem all to be as mad as the whole worshipful company of hatters,' he said bitterly, 'I suppose I *had* better take you home. But you're not to suppose I shall pass this over. I shall have something to say to you all tomorrow morning.'

'Yes, you will, my Lamb,' said Anthea under her breath, 'but it won't be at all the sort of thing you think it's going to be.'

In her heart she could hear the pretty, soft little loving voice of the baby Lamb – so different from the affected tones of the dreadful grown-up Lamb (one of whose names was Devereux) – saying, 'Me love Panty – wants to come to own Panty.'

'Oh, let's get home, for goodness' sake,' she said. 'You shall say whatever you like in the morning – if you can,' she added in a whisper.

It was a gloomy party that went home through the soft evening. During Anthea's remarks Robert had again made play with the pin and the bicycle tyre, and the Lamb (whom they had to call St Maur or Devereux or Hilary) seemed really at last to have had his fill of bicycle-mending. So the machine was wheeled.

The sun was just on the point of setting when they arrived at the White House. The four elder children would have liked to linger in the lane till the complete sunsetting turned the grown-up Lamb (whose Chistian names I will not further weary you by repeating) into their own dear tiresome baby brother. But he, in his grown-upness, insisted on going on, and thus he was met in the front garden by Martha.

Now you remember that, as a special favour, the Psammead had arranged that the servants in the house should never notice any change brought about by the wishes of the children. Therefore Martha merely saw the usual party, with the baby Lamb, about whom she had been desperately anxious all the afternoon, trotting beside Anthea on fat baby legs, while the children, of course, still saw the grown-up Lamb (never mind what names he was christened by), and Martha rushed at him and caught him in her arms, exclaiming:

'Come to his own Martha, then – a precious poppet!'

The grown-up Lamb (whose names shall now be buried in oblivion) struggled furiously. An expression of intense horror and annoyance was seen on his face. But Martha was stronger than he. She lifted him up and carried him into the house. None of the children will ever forget that picture. The neat grey-flannel-suited grown-up young man with the green tie and the little black moustache – fortunately, he was slightly built, and not tall – struggling in the sturdy arms of Martha, who bore him away helpless, imploring him, as she went, to be a good boy now, and come and have his nice bremmink! Fortunately, the sun set as they reached the doorstep, the bicycle disappeared, and Martha was seen to carry into the house the real live darling sleepy two-year-old Lamb. The grown-up Lamb (nameless henceforth) was gone for ever.

'For ever,' said Cyril, 'because, as soon as ever the Lamb's old enough to be bullied, we must jolly well begin to bully him, for his own sake – so that he mayn't grow up like *that*.'

'You shan't bully him,' said Anthea stoutly; 'not if I can stop it.'

'We must tame him by kindness,' said Jane.

'You see,' said Robert, 'if he grows up in the usual way, there'll be plenty of time to correct him as he goes along. The awful thing today was his growing up so suddenly. There was no time to improve him at all!'

'He doesn't want any improving,' said Anthea as the voice of the Lamb came coming through the open door, just as she had heard it in her heart that afternoon:

'Me loves Panty – wants to come to own Panty!'

Chapter X

SCALPS

Probably the day would have been a greater success if Cyril had not been reading *The Last of the Mohicans*. The story was running in his head at breakfast, and as he took his third cup of tea he said dreamily, 'I wish there were Red Indians in England – not big ones, you know, but little ones, just about the right size for us to fight.'

Everyone disagreed with him at the time, and no one attached any importance to the incident. But when they went down to the sand-pit to ask for a hundred pounds in two-shilling pieces with Queen Victoria's head on, to prevent mistakes – which they had always felt to be a really reasonable wish that must turn out well – they found that they had done it again! For the Psammead, which was very cross and sleepy, said:

'Oh, don't bother me. You've had your wish.'

'I didn't know it,' said Cyril.

'Don't you remember yesterday?' said the Sand-fairy, still more disagreeably. 'You asked me to let you have your wishes wherever you happened to be, and you wished this morning, and you've got it.'

'Oh, have we?' said Robert. 'What is it?'

'So you've forgotten?' said the Psammead, beginning to burrow. 'Never mind; you'll know soon enough. And I wish you joy of it! A nice thing you've let yourselves in for!'

'We always do, somehow,' said Jane sadly.

And now the odd thing was that no one could remember anyone's having wished for anything that morning. The wish about the Red Indians had not stuck in anyone's head. It was a most anxious morning. Everyone was trying to remember what had been wished for, and no one could, and everyone kept expecting something awful to happen every minute. It was most agitating; they knew, from what the Psammead had said, that they must have wished for something more than usually undesirable, and they spent several hours in most agonising uncertainty. It was not till nearly dinner-time that Jane tumbled over *The Last of the Mohicans* – which had, of course, been left face downwards on the floor – and when Anthea had picked her and the book up she suddenly said, 'I know!' and sat down flat on the carpet.

'Oh, Pussy, how awful! It was Indians he wished for – Cyril – at breakfast, don't you remember? He said, "I wish there were Red Indians in England," – and now there are, and they're going about scalping people all over the country, like as not.'

'Perhaps they're only in Northumberland and Durham,' said Jane soothingly. It was almost impossible to believe that it could really hurt people much to be scalped so far away as that.

'Don't you believe it!' said Anthea. 'The Sammyadd said we'd let ourselves in for a nice thing. That means they'll come *here*. And suppose they scalped the Lamb!'

'Perhaps the scalping would come right again at sunset,' said Jane; but she did not speak so hopefully as usual.

'Not it!' said Anthea. 'The things that grow out of the wishes don't go. Look at the fifteen shillings! Pussy, I'm going to break something, and you must let me have every penny of money you've got. The Indians will come *here*, don't you see? That spiteful Psammead as good as said so. You see what my plan is? Come on!'

Jane did not see at all. But she followed her sister meekly into their mother's bedroom.

Anthea lifted down the heavy water-jug – it had a pattern of storks and long grasses on it, which Anthea never forgot. She carried it into the dressing-room, and carefully emptied the water out of it into the bath. Then she took the jug back into the bed-room and dropped it on the floor. You know how a jug always breaks if you happen to drop it by accident. If you happen to drop it on purpose, it is quite different. Anthea dropped that jug three times, and it was as unbroken as ever. So at last she had to take her father's boot-tree and break the jug with that in cold blood. It was heartless work.

Next she broke open the missionary-box with the poker. Jane told her that it was wrong, of course, but Anthea shut her lips very tight and then said:

'Don't be silly – it's a matter of life and death.'

There was not very much in the missionary-box – only seven-and-fourpence – but the girls between them had nearly four shillings. This made over eleven shillings, as you will easily see.

Anthea tied the money in a corner of her pocket-handkerchief. 'Come on, Jane!' she said, and ran down to the farm. She knew that the farmer was going into Rochester that afternoon. In fact it had been arranged that he was to take the four children with him. They had planned this in the happy hour when they believed that they were going to get that hundred pounds, in two-shilling pieces, out of the Psammead. They had arranged to pay the farmer two shillings each for the ride. Now Anthea hastily explained to him that they could not go, but would he take Martha and Baby instead? He agreed, but he was not pleased to get only half-a-crown instead of eight shillings.

Then the girls ran home again. Anthea was agitated, but not flurried. When she came to think it over afterwards, she could not help seeing that she had acted with the most far-seeing promptitude, just like a born general. She fetched a little box from her corner drawer, and went to find Martha, who was laying the cloth and not in the best of tempers.

'Look here,' said Anthea. 'I've broken the toilet-jug in mother's room.'

'Just like you – always up to some mischief,' said Martha, dumping down a salt-cellar with a bang.

'Don't be cross, Martha dear,' said Anthea. 'I've got enough money to pay for a new one – if only you'll be a dear and go and buy it for us. Your cousins keep a china-shop, don't they? And I would like you to get it today, in case mother comes home tomorrow. You know she said she might, perhaps.'

'But you're all going into town yourselves,' said Martha.

'We can't afford to, if we get the new jug,' said Anthea; 'but we'll pay for you to go if you'll take the Lamb. And I say, Martha, look here – I'll give you my Liberty box, if you'll go. Look, it's most awfully pretty – all inlaid with real silver and ivory and ebony like King Solomon's temple.'

'I see,' said Martha; 'no, I don't want your box, miss. What you want is to get the precious Lamb off your hands for the afternoon. Don't you go for to think I don't see through you!'

This was so true that Anthea longed to deny it at once. Martha had no business to know so much. But she held her tongue.

Martha set down the bread with a bang that made it jump off its trencher.

'I *do* want the jug got,' said Anthea softly. 'You *will* go, won't you?'

'Well, just for this once, I don't mind; but mind you don't get into none of your outrageous mischief while I'm gone – that's all!'

'He's going earlier than he thought,' said Anthea eagerly. 'You'd better hurry and get dressed. Do put on that lovely purple frock, Martha, and the hat with the pink cornflowers, and the yellow-lace collar. Jane'll finish laying the cloth, and I'll wash the Lamb and get him ready.'

As she washed the unwilling Lamb, and hurried him into his best clothes, Anthea peeped out of the window from time to time;

so far all was well – she could see no Red Indians. When with a rush and a scurry and some deepening of the damask of Martha's complexion she and the Lamb had been got off, Anthea drew a deep breath.

'*He's* safe!' she said, and, to Jane's horror, flung herself down on the floor and burst into floods of tears. Jane did not understand at all how a person could be so brave and like a general, and then suddenly give way and go flat like an air-balloon when you prick it. It is better not to go flat, of course, but you will observe that Anthea did not give way till her aim was accomplished. She had got the dear Lamb out of danger – she felt certain the Red Indians would be round the White House or nowhere – the farmer's cart would not come back till after sunset, so she could afford to cry a little. It was partly with joy that she cried, because she had done what she meant to do. She cried for about three minutes, while Jane hugged her miserably and said at five-second intervals, 'Don't cry, Panther dear!'

Then she jumped up, rubbed her eyes hard with the corner of her pinafore, so that they kept red for the rest of the day, and started to tell the boys. But just at that moment cook rang the dinner-bell, and nothing could be said till they had all been helped to minced beef. Then cook left the room, and Anthea told her tale. But it is a mistake to tell a thrilling tale when people are eating minced beef and boiled potatoes. There seemed somehow to be something about the food that made the idea of Red Indians seem flat and unbelievable. The boys actually laughed, and called Anthea a little silly.

'Why,' said Cyril, 'I'm almost sure it was before I said that that Jane said she wished it would be a fine day.'

'It wasn't,' said Jane briefly.

'Why, if it was Indians,' Cyril went on – 'salt, please, and mustard – I must have something to make this mush go down – if it was Indians, they'd have been infesting the place long before this – you know they would. I believe it's the fine day.'

'Then why did the Sammyadd say we'd let ourselves in for a nice thing?' asked Anthea. She was feeling very cross. She knew she had acted with nobility and discretion, and after that it was very hard to be called a little silly, especially when she had the weight of a burgled missionary-box and about seven-and-fourpence, mostly in coppers, lying like lead upon her conscience.

There was a silence, during which cook took away the mincy plates and brought in the treacle-pudding. As soon as she had retired, Cyril began again.

'Of course I don't mean to say,' he admitted, 'that it wasn't a good thing to get Martha and the Lamb out of the light for the afternoon; but as for Red Indians – why, you know jolly well the wishes always come that very minute. If there was going to be Red Indians, they'd be here now.'

'I expect they are,' said Anthea; 'they're lurking amid the undergrowth, for anything you know. I do think you're most beastly unkind.'

'Indians almost always *do* lurk, really, though, don't they?' put in Jane, anxious for peace.

'No, they don't,' said Cyril tartly. 'And I'm not unkind, I'm only truthful. And I say it was utter rot breaking the water-jug; and as for the missionary-box, I believe it's a treason-crime, and I shouldn't wonder if you could be hanged for it, if any of us was to split –'

'Shut up, can't you?' said Robert; but Cyril couldn't. You see, he felt in his heart that if there *should* be Indians they would be entirely his own fault, so he did not wish to believe in them. And trying not to believe things when in your heart you are almost sure they are true, is as bad for the temper as anything I know.

'It's simply idiotic,' he said, 'talking about Indians, when you can see for yourselves that it's Jane who's got her wish. Look what a fine day it is – *OH!* –'

He had turned towards the window to point out the fineness of the day – the others turned too – and a frozen silence caught at Cyril, and none of the others felt at all like breaking it. For there, peering round the corner of the window, among the red leaves of the Virginia creeper, was a face – a brown face, with a long nose and a tight mouth and very bright eyes. And the face was painted in coloured patches. It had long black hair, and in the hair were feathers!

Every child's mouth in the room opened, and stayed open. The treacle-pudding was growing white and cold on their plates. No one could move.

Suddenly the feathered head was cautiously withdrawn, and the spell was broken. I am sorry to say that Anthea's first words were very like a girl.

'There, now!' she said. 'I told you so!'

Treacle-pudding had now definitely ceased to charm. Hastily wrapping their portions in a *Spectator* of the week before the week before last, they hid them behind the crinkled-paper stove-ornament, and fled upstairs to reconnoitre, and to hold a hurried council.

'Pax,' said Cyril handsomely when they reached their mother's bedroom. 'Panther, I'm sorry if I was a brute.'

'All right,' said Anthea, 'but you see now!'

No further trace of Indians, however, could be discerned from the windows.

'Well,' said Robert, 'what are we to do?'

'The only thing I can think of,' said Anthea, who was now generally admitted to be the heroine of the day, 'is – if we dressed up as like Indians as we can, and looked out of the windows, or even went out, they might think we were the powerful leaders of a neighbouring tribe, and – and not do anything to us, you know, for fear of awful vengeance.'

'But Eliza, and the cook?' said Jane.

'You forget – they can't notice anything,' said Robert. 'They wouldn't notice anything out of the way, even if they were scalped or roasted at a slow fire.'

'But would they come right at sunset?'

'Of course. You can't be really scalped or burned to death without noticing it, and you'd be sure to notice it next day, even if it escaped your attention at the time,' said Cyril. 'I think Anthea's right, but we shall want a most awful lot of feathers.'

'I'll go down to the hen-house,' said Robert.

'There's one of the turkeys in there – it's not very well. I could cut its feathers without it minding much. It's very bad – doesn't seem to care what happens to it. Get me the cutting-out scissors.'

Earnest reconnoitring convinced them all that no Indians were in the poultry-yard. Robert went. In five minutes he came back – pale, but with many feathers.

'Look here,' he said, 'this is jolly serious. I cut off the feathers, and when I turned to come out there was an Indian squinting at me from under the old hen-coop. I just brandished the feathers and yelled, and got away before he could get the coop off the top of himself. Panther, get the coloured blankets off our beds, and look slippy, can't you?'

It is wonderful how like an Indian you can make yourselves with blankets and feathers and coloured scarves. Of course none of the children happened to have long black hair, but there was a lot of black calico that had been got to cover school-books with. They cut strips of this into a sort of fine fringe, and fastened it round their heads with the amber-coloured ribbons off the girls' Sunday dresses. Then they stuck turkey's feathers in the ribbons. The calico looked very like long black hair, especially when the strips began to curl up a bit.

'But our faces,' said Anthea, 'they're not at all the right colour. We're all rather pale, and I'm sure I don't know why, but Cyril is the colour of putty.'

'I'm not,' said Cyril.

'The real Indians outside seem to be brownish,' said Robert

hastily. 'I think we ought to be really *red* – it's sort of superior to have a red skin, if you are one.'

The red ochre cook used for the kitchen bricks seemed to be about the reddest thing in the house. The children mixed some in a saucer with milk, as they had seen the cook do for the kitchen floor. Then they carefully painted each other's faces and hands with it, till they were quite as red as any Red Indian need be – if not redder.

They knew at once that they must look very terrible when they met Eliza in the passage, and she screamed aloud. This unsolicited testimonial pleased them very much. Hastily telling her not to be a goose, and that it was only a game, the four blanketed, feathered, really and truly Red-skins went boldly out to meet the foe. I say boldly. That is because I wish to be polite. At any rate, they went.

Along the hedge dividing the wilderness from the garden was a row of dark heads, all highly feathered.

'It's our only chance,' whispered Anthea. 'Much better than to wait for their blood-freezing attack. We must pretend like mad. Like that game of cards where you pretend you've got aces when you haven't. Fluffing they call it, I think. Now then, Whoop!'

With four wild war-whoops – or as near them as English children could be expected to go without any previous practice – they rushed through the gate and struck four warlike attitudes in the face of the line of Red Indians. These were all about the same height, and that height was Cyril's.

'I hope to goodness they can talk English,' said Cyril through his attitude.

Anthea knew they could, though she never knew how she came to know it. She had a white towel tied to a walking-stick. This was a flag of truce, and she waved it, in the hope that the Indians would know what it was. Apparently they did – for one who was browner than the others stepped forward.

'Ye seek a pow-wow?' he said in excellent English. 'I am Golden Eagle, of the mighty tribe of Rock-dwellers.'

'And I,' said Anthea, with a sudden inspiration, 'am the Black Panther – chief of the – the – the – Mazawattee tribe. My brothers – I don't mean – yes, I do – the tribe – I mean the Mazawattees – are in ambush below the brow of yonder hill.'

'And what mighty warriors be these?' asked Golden Eagle, turning to the others.

Cyril said he was the great chief Squirrel, of the Moning Congo tribe, and, seeing that Jane was sucking her thumb and could evidently think of no name for herself, he added, 'This great warrior is Wild Cat – Pussy Ferox we call it in this land – leader of the vast Phiteezi tribe.'

'And thou, valorous Redskin?' Golden Eagle inquired suddenly of Robert, who, taken unawares, could only reply that he was Bobs, leader of the Cape Mounted Police.

'And now,' said Black Panther, 'our tribes, if we just whistle them up, will far outnumber your puny forces; so resistance is useless. Return, therefore, to your own land, O brother, and smoke pipes of peace in your wampums with your squaws and your medicine-men, and dress yourself in the gayest wigwams, and eat happily of the juicy fresh-caught moccasins.'

'You've got it all wrong,' murmured Cyril angrily. But Golden Eagle only looked inquiringly at her.

'Thy customs are other than ours, O Black Panther,' he said. 'Bring up thy tribe, that we may hold pow-wow in state before them, as becomes great chiefs.'

'We'll bring them up right enough,' said Anthea, 'with their bows and arrows, and tomahawks and scalping-knives, and everything you can think of, if you don't look sharp and go.'

She spoke bravely enough, but the hearts of all the children were beating furiously, and their breath came in shorter and shorter gasps. For the little Red Indians were closing up round them – coming nearer and nearer with angry murmurs – so that they were the centre of a crowd of dark cruel faces.

'It's no go,' whispered Robert. 'I knew it wouldn't be. We must make a bolt for the Psammead. It might help us. If it doesn't – well, I suppose we shall come alive again at sunset. I wonder if scalping hurts as much as they say.'

'I'll wave the flag again,' said Anthea. 'If they stand back, we'll run for it.'

She waved the towel, and the chief commanded his followers to stand back. Then, charging wildly at the place where the line of Indians was thinnest, the four children started to run. Their first rush knocked down some half-dozen Indians, over whose blanketed bodies the children leaped, and made straight for the sand-pit. This was no time for the safe easy way by which carts go down – right over the edge of the sand-pit they went, among the yellow and pale purple flowers and dried grasses, past the little sand-martins' little front doors, skipping, clinging, bounding, stumbling, sprawling, and finally rolling.

Yellow Eagle and his followers came up with them just at the very spot where they had seen the Psammead that morning.

Breathless and beaten, the wretched children now awaited their fate. Sharp knives and axes gleamed round them, but worse than these was the cruel light in the eyes of Golden Eagle and his followers.

'Ye have lied to us, O Black Panther of the Mazawattees – and thou, too, Squirrel of the Moning Congos. These also, Pussy Ferox of the Phiteezi, and Bobs of the Cape Mounted Police, – these also have lied to us, if not with their tongues, yet by their silence. Ye have lied under the cover of the Truce-flag of the Paleface. Ye have no followers. Your tribes are far away – following the hunting trail. What shall be their doom?' he concluded, turning with a bitter smile to the other Red Indians.

'Build we the fire!' shouted his followers; and at once a dozen ready volunteers started to look for fuel. The four children, each held between two strong little Indians, cast despairing glances round them. Oh, if they could only see the Psammead!

'Do you really mean to scalp us first and then roast us?' asked Anthea desperately.

'Of course!' Redskin opened his eyes at her. 'It's always done.'

The Indians had formed a ring round the children, and now sat on the ground gazing at their captives. There was a threatening silence.

Then slowly, by twos and threes, the Indians who had gone to look for firewood came back, and they came back empty-handed. They had not been able to find a single stick of wood for a fire! No one ever can, as a matter of fact, in that part of Kent.

The children drew a deep breath of relief, but it ended in a moan of terror. For bright knives were being brandished all about them. Next moment each child was seized by an Indian; each closed its eyes and tried not to scream. They waited for the sharp agony of the knife. It did not come. Next moment they were released, and fell in a trembling heap. Their heads did not hurt at all. They only felt strangely cool! Wild war-whoops rang in their ears. When they ventured to open their eyes they saw four of their foes dancing round them with wild leaps and screams, and each of the four brandished in his hand a scalp of long flowing black hair. They put their hands to their heads – their own scalps were safe! The poor untutored savages had indeed scalped the children. But they had only, so to speak, scalped them of the black calico ringlets!

The children fell into each other's arms, sobbing and laughing.

'Their scalps are ours,' chanted the chief; 'ill-rooted were their ill-fated hairs! They came off in the hands of the victors – without struggle, without resistance, they yielded their scalps to the conquering Rock-dwellers! Oh, how little a thing is a scalp so lightly won!'

'They'll take our real ones in a minute; you see if they don't,' said Robert, trying to rub some of the red ochre off his face and hands on to his hair.

'Cheated of our just and fiery revenge are we,' the chant went on, – 'but there are other torments than the scalping-knife and the flames. Yet is the slow fire the correct thing. O strange unnatural country, wherein a man may find no wood to burn his enemy – Ah, for the boundless forests of my native land, where the great trees for thousands of miles grow but to furnish firewood where-withal to burn our foes. Ah, would we were but in our native forest once more!'

Suddenly, like a flash of lightning, the golden gravel shone all round the four children instead of the dusky figures. For every single Indian had vanished on the instant at their leader's word. The Psammead must have been there all the time. And it had given the Indian chief his wish.

·   ·   ·

Martha brought home a jug with a pattern of storks and long grasses on it. Also she brought back all Anthea's money.

'My cousin, she give me the jug for luck; she said it was an odd one what the basin of had got smashed.'

'Oh, Martha, you are a dear!' sighed Anthea, throwing her arms round her.

'Yes,' giggled Martha, 'you'd better make the most of me while you've got me. I shall give your ma notice directly minute she comes back.'

'Oh, Martha, we haven't been so *very* horrid to you, have we?' asked Anthea, aghast.

'No, it ain't that, miss.' Martha giggled more than ever. 'I'm a-goin' to be married. It's Beale the gamekeeper. He's been aproposin' to me off and on ever since you come home from the clergyman's where you got locked up on the church-tower. And today I said the word an' made him a happy man.'

Anthea put the seven-and-fourpence back in the missionary-box, and pasted paper over the place where the poker had broken it. She was very glad to be able to do this, and she does not know to this day whether breaking open a missionary-box is or is not a hanging matter.

Chapter XI (and last)

THE LAST WISH

Of course you, who see above that this is the eleventh (and last) chapter, know very well that the day of which this chapter tells must be the last on which Cyril, Anthea, Robert and Jane will have a chance of getting anything out of the Psammead, or Sand-fairy.

But the children themselves did not know this. They were full of rosy visions, and, whereas on other days they had often found it extremely difficult to think of anything really nice to wish for, their brains were now full of the most beautiful and sensible ideas. 'This,' as Jane remarked afterwards, 'is always the way.' Everyone was up extra early that morning, and these plans were hopefully discussed in the garden before breakfast. The old idea of one hundred pounds in modern florins was still first favourite, but there were others that ran it close – the chief of these being the 'pony each' idea. This had a great advantage. You could wish for a pony each during the morning, ride it all day, have it vanish at sunset and wish it back again next day. Which would be an economy of litter and stabling. But at breakfast two things happened. First, there was a letter from mother. Granny was better, and mother and father hoped to be home that very afternoon. A cheer arose. And of course this news at once scattered all the before-breakfast wish-ideas. For everyone saw quite plainly that the wish of the day must be something to please mother and not to please themselves.

'I wonder what she *would* like,' pondered Cyril.

'She'd like us all to be good,' said Jane primly.

'Yes – but that's so dull for us,' Cyril rejoined; 'and, besides, I should hope we could be that without sand-fairies to help us. No; it must be something splendid, that we couldn't possibly get without wishing for.'

'Look out,' said Anthea in a warning voice; 'don't forget yesterday. Remember, we get our wishes now just wherever we happen to be when we say "I wish." Don't let's let ourselves in for anything silly – today of all days.'

'All right,' said Cyril. 'You needn't jaw.'

Just then Martha came in with a jug full of hot water for the teapot – and a face full of importance for the children.

'A blessing we're all alive to eat our breakfasses!' she said darkly.

'Why, whatever's happened?' everybody asked.

'Oh, nothing,' said Martha, 'only it seems nobody's safe from being murdered in their beds nowadays.'

'Why,' said Jane as an agreeable thrill of horror ran down her back and legs and out at her toes, '*has* anyone been murdered in their beds?'

'Well – not exactly,' said Martha; 'but they might just as well. There's been burglars over at Peasmarsh Place – Beale's just told me – and they've took every single one of Lady Chittenden's diamonds and jewels and things, and she's a-goin' out of one fainting fit into another, with hardly time to say "Oh, my diamonds!" in between. And Lord Chittenden's away in London.'

'Lady Chittenden,' said Anthea; 'we've seen her. She wears a red-and-white dress, and she has no children of her own and can't abide other folkses'.'

'That's her,' said Martha. 'Well, she's put all her trust in riches, and you see how she's served. They say the diamonds and things was worth thousands of thousands of pounds. There was a necklace and a river – whatever that is – and no end of bracelets; and a tarrer and ever so many rings. But there, I mustn't stand talking and all the place to clean down afore your ma comes home.'

'I don't see why she should ever have had such a lot of diamonds,' said Anthea when Martha had flounced off. 'She was rather a nasty lady, I thought. And mother hasn't any diamonds, and hardly any jewels – the topaz necklace, and the sapphire ring daddy gave her when they were engaged, and the garnet star, and the little pearl brooch with great-grandpapa's hair in it – that's about all.'

'When I'm grown up I'll buy mother no end of diamonds,' said Robert, 'if she wants them. I shall make so much money exploring Africa I shan't know what to do with it.'

'Wouldn't it be jolly,' said Jane dreamily, 'if mother could find all those lovely things, necklaces and rivers of diamonds and tarrers?'

'*Ti–aras,*' said Cyril.

'Ti–aras, then – and rings and everything in her room when she came home? I wish she could.'

The others gazed at her in horror.

'Well, she *will*,' said Robert; 'you've wished, my good Jane – and our only chance now is to find the Psammead, and if it's in a good temper it *may* take back the wish and give us another. If not – well – goodness knows what we're in for! – the police, of course, and – Don't cry, silly! We'll stand by you. Father says we need never be afraid if we don't do anything wrong and always speak the truth.'

But Cyril and Anthea exchanged gloomy glances. They remembered how convincing the truth about the Psammead had been once before when told to the police.

It was a day of misfortunes. Of course the Psammead could not be found. Nor the jewels, though every one of the children searched their mother's room again and again.

'Of course,' Robert said, '*we* couldn't find them. It'll be Mother who'll do that. Perhaps she'll think they've been in the house for years and years, and never know they are stolen ones at all.'

'Oh yes!' Cyril was very scornful; 'then Mother will be a receiver of stolen goods, and you know jolly well what *that's* worse than.'

Another and exhaustive search of the sand-pit failed to reveal the Psammead, so the children went back to the house slowly and sadly.

'I don't care,' said Anthea stoutly, 'we'll tell mother the truth, and she'll give back the jewels – and make everything all right.'

'Do you think so?' said Cyril slowly. 'Do you think she'll believe us? Could anyone believe about a Sammyadd unless they'd seen it? She'll think we're pretending. Or else she'll think we're raving mad, and then we shall be sent to Bedlam. How would you like it?' – he turned suddenly on the miserable Jane – 'how would you like it, to be shut up in an iron cage with bars and padded walls, and nothing to do but stick straws in your hair all day, and listen to the howling and ravings of the other maniacs? Make up your minds to it, all of you. It's no use telling mother.'

'But it's true,' said Jane.

'Of course it is, but it's not true enough for grown-up people to believe it,' said Anthea. 'Cyril's right. Let's put flowers in all the vases, and try not to think about diamonds. After all, everything has come right in the end all the other times.'

So they filled all the pots they could find with flowers – asters and zinnias, and loose-leaved late red roses from the wall of the stable-yard, till the house was a perfect bower.

And almost as soon as dinner was cleared away Mother arrived, and was clasped in eight loving arms. It was very difficult indeed not to tell her all about the Psammead at once, because they had got into the habit of telling her everything. But they did succeed in not telling her.

Mother, on her side, had plenty to tell them – about Granny, and Granny's pigeons, and Auntie Emma's lame tame donkey. She was very delighted with the flowery-boweryness of the house; and everything seemed so natural and pleasant, now that she was home again, that the children almost thought they must have dreamed the Psammead.

But, when Mother moved towards the stairs to go up to her bedroom and take off her bonnet, the eight arms clung round her just as if she only had two children, one the Lamb and the other an octopus.

'Don't go up, Mummy darling,' said Anthea, 'let me take your things up for you.'

'Or I will,' said Cyril.

'We want you to come and look at the rose-tree,' said Robert.

'Oh, don't go up!' said Jane helplessly.

'Nonsense, dears,' said Mother briskly, 'I'm not such an old woman yet that I can't take my bonnet off in the proper place. Besides, I must wash these black hands of mine.'

So up she went, and the children, following her, exchanged glances of gloomy foreboding.

Mother took off her bonnet – it was a very pretty hat, really, with white roses in it – and when she had taken it off she went to the dressing-room to do her pretty hair.

On the table between the ring-stand and the pin-cushion lay a green leather case. Mother opened it.

'Oh, how lovely!' she cried. It was a ring, a large pearl with shining many-lighted diamonds set round it. 'Wherever did this come from?' mother asked, trying it on her wedding finger, which it fitted beautifully. 'However did it come here?'

'I don't know,' said each of the children truthfully.

'Father must have told Martha to put it here,' Mother said. 'I'll run down and ask her.'

'Let me look at it,' said Anthea, who knew Martha would not be able to see the ring. But when Martha was asked, of course she denied putting the ring there, and so did Eliza and the cook.

Mother came back to her bedroom, very much interested and pleased about the ring. But, when she opened the dressing-table drawer and found a long case containing an almost priceless diamond necklace, she was more interested still, though not so pleased. In the wardrobe, when she went to put away her 'bonnet', she found a tiara and several brooches, and the rest of the jewellery turned up in various parts of the room during the next half-hour. The children looked more and more uncomfortable, and now Jane began to sniff.

Mother looked at her gravely.

'Jane,' she said, 'I am sure you know something about this. Now think before you speak, and tell me the truth.'

'We found a Fairy,' said Jane obediently.

'No nonsense, please,' said her mother sharply.

'Don't be silly, Jane,' Cyril interrupted. Then he went on desperately. 'Look here, Mother, we've never seen the things before, but Lady Chittenden at Peasmarsh Place lost all her jewellery by wicked burglars last night. Could this possibly be it?'

All drew a deep breath. They were saved.

'But how could they have put it here? And why should they?' asked Mother, not unreasonanbly. 'Surely it would have been easier and safer to make off with it?'

'Suppose,' said Cyril, 'they thought it better to wait for – for supper – nightfall, I mean, before they went off with it. No one but us knew that you were coming back today.'

'I must send for the police at once,' said Mother distractedly. 'Oh, how I wish Daddy were here!'

'Wouldn't it be better to wait till he *does* come?' asked Robert, knowing that his father would not come home before sunset.

'No, no; I can't wait a minute with all this on my mind,' cried Mother. 'All this' was the heap of jewel-cases on the bed. They put them all in the wardrobe, and mother locked it. Then Mother called Martha.

'Martha,' she said, 'has any stranger been into my room since I've been away? Now, answer me truthfully.'

'No, mum,' answered Martha; 'leastways, what I mean to say –' She stopped.

'Come,' said her mistress kindly; 'I see someone has. You must tell me at once. Don't be frightened. I'm sure you haven't done anything wrong.'

Martha burst into heavy sobs.

'I was a-goin' to give you warning this very day, mum, to leave at the end of my month, so I was, – on account of me being going to make a respectable young man happy. A gamekeeper he is by trade, mum – and I wouldn't deceive you – of the name of Beale. And it's as true as I stand here, it was your coming home in such a hurry, and no warning given, out of the kindness of his heart it was, as he says, "Martha, my beauty," he says – which I ain't, and never was, but you know how them men will go on – "I can't see you a-toiling and a-moiling and not lend a 'helping 'and; which mine is a strong arm and it's yours, Martha, my dear," says he. And so he helped me a-cleanin' of the windows – but outside, mum, the whole time, and me in; if I never say another breathing word it's the gospel truth.'

'Were you with him the whole time?' asked her mistress.

'Him outside, me in, I was,' said Martha; 'except for fetching up a fresh pail and the leather that that slut of a Eliza'd hidden away behind the mangle.'

'That will do,' said the children's mother. 'I am not pleased with you, Martha, but you have spoken the truth, and that counts for something.'

When Martha had gone, the children clung round their mother.

'Oh, Mummy darling,' cried Anthea, 'it isn't Beale's fault, it isn't, really! He's a great dear; he is, truly and honourably, and as honest as the day. Don't let the police take him, Mummy! oh, don't, don't, don't.'

It was truly awful. Here was an innocent man accused of robbery through that silly wish of Jane's, and it was absolutely useless to tell the truth. All longed to, but they thought of the straws in the hair and the shrieks of the other frantic maniacs, and they could not do it.

'Is there a cart hereabouts?' asked Mother feverishly. 'A trap of any sort? I must drive in to Rochester and tell the police at once.'

All the children sobbed, 'There's a cart at the farm, but, oh, don't go! – don't go! – oh, don't go! – wait till daddy comes home!'

Mother took not the faintest notice. When she had set her mind on a thing she always went straight through with it; she was rather like Anthea in this respect.

'Look here, Cyril,' she said, sticking on her hat with long sharp violet-headed pins, 'I leave you in charge. Stay in the dressing-room. You can pretend to be swimming boats in the bath, or something. Say I gave you leave. But stay here, with the landing door open; I've locked the other. And don't let anyone go into my room. Remember, no one knows the jewels are there except me, and all of you, and the wicked thieves who put them there. Robert, you stay in the garden and watch the windows. If anyone tries to get in you must run and tell the two farm men that I'll send up to wait in the kitchen. I'll tell them there are dangerous characters about – that's true enough. Now, remember, I trust you both. But I don't think they'll try it till after dark, so you're quite safe. Good-bye, darlings.'

And she locked her bedroom door and went off with the key in her pocket.

The children could not help admiring the dashing and decided way in which she had acted. They thought how useful she would have been in organising escape from some of the tight places in which they had found themselves of late in consequence of their ill-timed wishes.

'She's a born general,' said Cyril – 'but I don't know what's going to happen to us. Even if the girls were to hunt for that beastly Sammyadd and find it, and get it to take the jewels away again, Mother would only think we hadn't looked out properly and let the burglars sneak in and nick them – or else the police will think *we've* got them – or else that she's been fooling them. Oh, it's a pretty decent average ghastly mess this time, and no mistake!'

He savagely made a paper boat and began to float it in the bath, as he had been told to do.

Robert went into the garden and sat down on the worn yellow grass, with his miserable head between his helpless hands.

Anthea and Jane whispered together in the passage downstairs, where the coconut matting was – with the whole in it that you always caught your foot in if you were not careful. Martha's voice could be heard in the kitchen – grumbling loud and long.

'It's simply quite too dreadfully awful,' said Anthea. 'How do you know all the diamonds are there, too? If they aren't the police will think Mother and Father have got them, and that they've only given up some of them for a kind of desperate blind. And they'll be put in prison, and we shall be branded outcasts, the children of felons. And it won't be at all nice for Father and Mother either,' she added, by a candid afterthought.

'But what can we *do*?' asked Jane.

'Nothing – at least we might look for the Psammead again. It's a very, *very* hot day. He may have come out to warm that whisker of his.'

'He won't give us any more beastly wishes today,' said Jane

flatly. 'He gets crosser and crosser every time we see him. I believe he hates having to give wishes.'

Anthea had been shaking her head gloomily – now she stopped shaking it so suddenly that it really looked as though she were pricking up her ears.

'What is it?' asked Jane. 'Oh, have you thought of something?'

'Our one chance,' cried Anthea dramatically; 'the last lone-lorn forlorn hope. Come on.'

At a brisk trot she led the way to the sand-pit.

Oh, joy! – there was the Psammead, basking in a golden sandy hollow and preening its whiskers happily in the glowing afternoon sun. The moment it saw them it whisked round and began to burrow – it evidently preferred its own company to theirs. But Anthea was too quick for it. She caught it by its furry shoulders gently but firmly, and held it.

'Here – none of that!' said the Psammead. 'Leave go of me, will you?'

But Anthea held him fast.

'Dear kind darling Sammyadd,' she said breathlessly.

'Oh yes – it's all very well,' it said; 'you want another wish, I expect. But I can't keep on slaving from morning till night giving people their wishes. I must have *some* time to myself.'

'Do you hate giving wishes?' asked Anthea gently, and her voice trembled with excitement.

'Of course I do,' it said. 'Leave go of me or I'll bite! – I really will – I mean it. Oh, well, if you choose to risk it.'

Anthea risked it and held on.

'Look here,' she said, 'don't bite me – listen to reason. If you'll only do what we want today, we'll never ask you for another wish as long as we live.'

The Psammead was much moved.

'I'd do anything,' it said in a tearful voice. 'I'd almost burst myself to give you one wish after another, as long as I held out, if you'd only never, never ask me to do it after today. If you knew how I hate to blow myself out with other people's wishes, and how frightened I am always that I shall strain a muscle or something. And then to wake up every morning and know you've *got* to do it. You don't know what it is – you don't know what it is, you don't!' Its voice cracked with emotion, and the last 'don't' was a squeak.

Anthea set it down gently on the sand.

'It's all over now,' she said soothingly. 'We promise faithfully never to ask for another wish after today.'

'Well, go ahead,' said the Psammead; 'let's get it over.'

'How many can you do?'

'I don't know – as long as I can hold out.'

'Well, first, I wish Lady Chittenden may find she's never lost her jewels.'

The Psammead blew itself out, collapsed, and said, 'Done.'

'I wish,' said Anthea more slowly, 'Mother mayn't get to the police.'

'Done,' said the creature after the proper interval.

'I wish,' said Jane suddenly, 'Mother could forget all about the diamonds.'

'Done,' said the Psammead; but its voice was weaker.

'Wouldn't you like to rest a little?' asked Anthea considerately.

'Yes, please,' said the Psammead; 'and before we go any further, will you wish something for me?'

'Can't you do wishes for yourself?'

'Of course not,' it said; 'we were always expected to give each other our wishes – not that we had any to speak of in the good old Megatherium days. Just wish, will you, that you may never be able, any of you, to tell anyone a word about *me*.'

'Why?' asked Jane.

'Why, don't you see, if you told grown-ups I should have no peace in my life. They'd get hold of me, and they wouldn't wish silly things like you do, but real earnest things; and the scientific people would hit on some ways of making things last after sunset, as likely as not; and they'd ask for a graduated income-tax, and old-age pensions, and manhood suffrage, and free secondary education, and dull things like that; and get them, and keep them, and the whole world would be turned topsy-turvy. Do wish it! Quick!'

Anthea repeated the Psammead's wish, and it blew itself out to a larger size than they had yet seen it attain.

'And now,' it said as it collapsed, 'can I do anything more for you?'

'Just one thing; and I think that clears everything up, doesn't it, Jane? I wish Martha to forget about the diamond ring, and Mother to forget about the keeper cleaning the windows.'

'It's like the "Brass Bottle",' said Jane.

'Yes, I'm glad we read that or I should never have thought of it.'

'Now,' said the Psammead faintly, 'I'm almost worn out. Is there anything else?'

'No; only thank you kindly for all you've done for us, and I hope you'll have a good long sleep, and I hope we shall see you again some day.'

'Is that a wish?' it said in a weak voice.

'Yes, please,' said the two girls together.

Then for the last time in this story they saw the Psammead blow itself out and collapse suddenly. It nodded to them, blinked its long snail's eyes, burrowed, and disappeared, scratching fiercely to the last, and the sand closed over it.

'I hope we've done right?' said Jane.

'I'm sure we have,' said Anthea. 'Come on home and tell the boys.'

Anthea found Cyril glooming over his paper boats, and told him. Jane found Robert. The two tales were only just ended when Mother walked in, hot and dusty. She explained that as she was being driven into Rochester to buy the girls' autumn school-dresses the axle had broken, and but for the narrowness of the lane and the high soft hedges she would have been thrown out. As it was, she was not hurt, but she had had to walk home. 'And oh, my dearest dear chicks,' she said, 'I am simply dying for a cup of tea! Do run and see if the kettle boils!'

'So you see it's all right,' Jane whispered. 'She doesn't remember.'

'No more does Martha,' said Anthea, who had been to ask about the state of the kettle.

As the servants sat at their tea, Beale the gamekeeper dropped in. He brought the welcome news that Lady Chittenden's diamonds had not been lost at all. Lord Chittenden had taken them to be re-set and cleaned, and the maid who knew about it had gone for a holiday. So that was all right.

'I wonder if we ever shall see the Psammead again,' said Jane wistfully as they walked in the garden, while mother was putting the Lamb to bed.

'I'm sure we shall,' said Cyril, 'if you really wished it.'

'We've promised never to ask it for another wish,' said Anthea.

'I never want to,' said Robert earnestly.

They did see it again, of course, but not in this story. And it was not in a sand-pit either, but in a very, very, very different place. It was in a – But I must say no more.

EXPLICIT